AVENGING SPIRIT

VALE INVESTIGATION, BOOK THREE

CRISTELLE COMBY

ALSO BY CRISTELLE COMBY

The Neve & Egan Cases

RUSSIAN DOLLS

RUBY HEART

DANSE MACABRE

BLIND CHESS

Vale Investigation

HOSTILE TAKEOVER

EVIL EMBERS

AVENGING SPIRIT

Short Stories

Personal Favour (*Neve & Egan* prequel)

Redemption Road (*Vale Investigation* prequel)

The short stories are exclusively available on the author's website:

www.cristelle-comby.com/freebooks

Edition: 1

ISBN: 978-1713196235

Credits
Editor: Johnathon Haney
Cover artist: Miguel A. Ereza

CELL OF THE RISING SUN

I should have been dead, but that wasn't the case just yet.

I groaned as I flexed my shoulder, aching from the bullet it took a few minutes ago. The gesture sent hot spikes of pain shooting through my nervous system. Damn, but it hurt.

Some fools might think signing a compact with Death Incarnate to become her envoy in the mortal realm is a good thing. I beg to differ.

"Moron," I muttered, gazing through the iron bars of the cell I was locked in. "Always read the fine print."

If I had, I might have noticed the immortality clause on the contract lacked the pain-free option. Then again, seeing as I had to be told about the immortality thing after the fact...

I shook my head and turned away from the barren concrete floor around the cell, leaning back against the cold metal bars. It didn't do squat to alleviate the pain, but I was bleeding from a gunshot wound—I didn't expect it to.

The bullet—a nine-mil, by my estimate—tore through my

flesh and muscle at an impossible angle. As if by sheer luck, the little piece of lead managed to miss all my major arteries and bones on its way through. Mind you, I'd rather it missed me completely, but avoiding pain hadn't been put in whatever passed for my boss's day planner. Hells if I knew what Lady McDeath was mad at me for this time.

Glancing down to check the wound, I realized the bleeding had stopped. My boosted immune system had kicked into overdrive, ensuring I would once again make a full—if improbable—recovery. Of course, the wound wouldn't heal itself in the blink of an eye, but my shoulder should be as good as new in a matter of days. A trip to the ER could go a long way towards speeding up the healing process, but considering how this day was unfolding, it seemed like it was one more injury that would have to heal on its own.

The cell I was stuck in was tiny. All four sides of those firm metal bars stretched no more than three feet across and the only accessory in it was an old, worn-out cot that was tossed in the back. Currently, a twenty-something Japanese woman was occupying that cot, out cold.

I moved my eyes over to the left and found the locked door. It had the same iron bars as the rest of our cell, held in place by thick, sturdy hinges of the same metal. My kingdom for a hacksaw...

Seeing nothing else interesting, I slid my eyes over to my fellow prisoner. Her lithe, little body was snugged inside loose black trousers and a matching, tight-fitting shirt with long sleeves. Her shoulder-length dark hair was a tangled mess that covered a large portion of her face, hiding most of the porcelain white skin underneath it.

As I looked her over, I noticed a pronounced streak of

red crossing through the black hair on her right side, which made me frown.

Was this kind of hair dye a new trend with the kids these days? I shook my head again, this time in reproach. Bah, what did I know about it anyways? With my combat boots, cargo pants and M65 field jacket, I was hardly the right person to be lecturing anybody on the topic of fashion, even if my last big case had involved a lot of it.

I turned my attention back to taking stock of our situation. Every time I did, I kept coming to the same conclusion. Since I didn't know any of my captors, there was no way I could trick my way out of here. And seeing as they'd taken both my gun and knife before locking us up, there was no way I could force my way out, either.

Frustrated, I slapped at the nearest bar with my bad arm and groaned when it woke up my wounded shoulder.

The pain wasn't the only thing my groan woke up; the young woman in the cot moaned as her eyes fluttered open. She rose out of her sleeping position by pushing herself up onto her elbows. She stared at the same concrete floor and metal bars that I had with a deepening frown. She saw me by the door and froze.

"Who the hell are you?" she asked. There wasn't a hint of an accent in her voice, not even of the American variety.

I raised my hands, making sure both palms faced her. "It's okay. I'm a friend."

Going by the way her dark, almond-shaped eyes narrowed, she didn't believe either sentence. "Who. Are. You?" she repeated, making each word its own separate sentence.

"The name's Vale...Bellamy Vale." Seeing as my

shoulder was acting up again, I lowered my hands before going on with, "I'm a private investigator."

She took a second to consider my answer. Glancing around the cage we were stuck in, she snorted. "Not a good one."

I chuckled as I turned on my best Cheshire Cat smile. "See, that's where I beg to differ, Yukina."

As expected, the use of her first name shook her enough to give me a harder stare. To prevent any misunderstandings, I went on with, "I was hired to find you—" I motioned at her with my hand. "—and I did. So, in my book, that makes me a really good P.I."

Her thin nose twitched as she pursed her lips, the shock giving way to annoyance. "So...the both of us getting locked up in here was all part of your master plan? Nice to know." She sat up fully. "Care to tell me what's the next step, Mr. Vale?"

I kept the smile up but it lost some of its wattage. "I'll, uh, have to get back to you on that."

She rolled her eyes at me before patting herself down.

"Don't bother," I told her. "They did a thorough frisk on the both of us while you were out. They got all your blades, along with my weapons."

That factoid didn't stop her from checking herself over. At last, she reached the hem of her left sleeve and smiled. "You can always count on the idiots to overlook something."

Her fingers played with the hem. At the push of her thumb, a thin needle popped its way out of the stitches. One of my eyebrows popped up as well. Seemed like she'd be rescuing me instead of the other way around.

Standing up in one swift, fluid motion, Yukina went over

to the door and knelt down. The needle between her fingers was thin but more than long enough to reach inside the locking mechanism. I could hear it pick through the tumblers with the delicacy of a concert pianist playing Beethoven. While she was working on our exit, I gave the space outside our cell another look.

The walls were made of the same dusty concrete as the floor, making me think we were below street level. No visible cameras were monitoring us, but there could always be high-tech versions that blended in with the scenery. The only distinguishing feature about this room, aside from the cell, was the single light bulb hanging from a wire in its center.

Not very *Feng Shui*, I thought to myself. That's when I remembered my hosts were Japanese. If they practiced anything, it would likely be *Fusui*—not that I thought they did, going by all this.

I turned my gaze back to the cell door to see how close Yukina was to getting us free. It wasn't long until I heard a familiar metallic click. That sweet sound told me that she'd managed to jam the needle in the right spot. She gave it a good twist and—*clang*—the cell door unlocked. Two seconds later, the wooden door on the other side of the room opened up, which made me tense.

Five Japanese men stepped into the room in single file. The first two had their pistols in hand, aiming at us the instant we were in their line of sight. By the time they staked out their firing positions, the other three had entered the room, their own firing hands resting inches away from their hip holsters.

I'd seen men like these before. Hells, a lifetime ago, I'd been one. The way they moved and held themselves all but screamed "private security firm". I didn't need to read their CV to know their general profile: young, athletic, extensive knowledge of weaponry and hand-to-hand combat, possibly ex-military. They all wore matching suits that were a cross between business casual and formal office wear, with jackets the perfect length to conceal the weapons at their sides. The dark colors and tight fit on them would allow these guys to blend into everyday environments while still giving them a broad range of motion.

The only odd, attention-grabbing detail on them was the tattoo they all had on the back of their right hand. It was some sort of Japanese symbol inked in black, right between the knuckles and wrist. Something about it made me think of cattle branding.

Yukina spat something to them in Japanese. Even if I knew any of the language beyond "thank you", "yes" and "hi", I'd still have had trouble deciphering the words through her rapid delivery. When no response came, she repeated her question, spitting it out twice as fast as before. Silence was her only answer and she huffed at them indignantly.

I stole a glance at her. Yukina was standing behind the cell door, the needle stowed somewhere out of sight. She looked every bit the caged animal they thought she was. Our sole ace up the sleeve was the fact that the cell was now unlocked. We'd have to wait until we could make the most of that advantage. In situations like this, patience was your best friend, with timing being a close second. I was glad to see that, for all her fury, Yukina seemed to know this as well as I did.

I was working out the next step in the plan I'd promised her when a sixth figure entered the room. This man had nothing in common with the armed goons. His short, round body was fitted in an expensive suit—Armani, or something as pricy. He had a thin mustache and round glasses that rested on a small nose set in the middle of his equally roly-poly face. Hells, even his haircut—a classic Beatles-style bowl cut—added to the overall air of roundness he had about him. The fat in his cheeks made him look young, but I put his actual age at between forty and fifty. I couldn't stop my lips from curling up at the sight of him; he looked like a hot air balloon with legs in place of the basket.

"Ms. Tsing, Mr. Vale," the newcomer said, in a nasal voice higher-pitched than his thick frame suggested. "So glad to see you both awake. Tell me...how do you like your new accommodations?"

"Two stars at best," I quipped with a cheeky grin. "You should consider installing a mini-bar."

His lips twitched into something that didn't pretend to be a smile. I wasn't offended. Plenty of people don't get my sense of humor.

"What do you want, Kung?" Yukina asked, her tone cold and crisp.

"Ah, straight to the point," Kung, said as he got within two feet of the cell door. "I appreciate that when it comes to business transactions."

She gave him the same glare she'd given me. "I'm not here to do business with you."

He responded with something that resembled a benevolent smile. "Oh, but you are, Ms. Tsing, you most certainly are."

He turned to the side and paced back and forth. I was doing calculations on how fast I could open the door when he got close to us again. "See, everything in this life is a business transaction of one kind or another. Buying and selling, favors and debts." He stopped pacing short of the cell door to raise a fat sausage-like finger. "And you, young lady, are now very much indebted to me. It is time to even that balance."

"Go to hell!" Yukina spat out, doing some pacing of her own. Judging from the tension I saw in her movements, it was taking everything she had not to lash out at him.

"Given your current situation, Ms. Tsing, one could argue that you and your associate are already there," Kung said, dropping the fake smile for actual menace.

He got closer to the cell door with slow, deliberate steps. "You have no idea how much trouble you've got yourself into, do you?"

Hells, yet another crime boss who's having a torrid love affair with the sound of his own voice, I thought wryly. The late, unlamented Alonzo Vitorini was bad enough.

"See, I could ask any of these gentlemen by my side to kill you right now," he went on. "I have the option on how quickly I want it to happen. And then, when your precious uncle opens up his shop tomorrow morning, he would find your body—or what is left of it—laying on the stoop. And that would be that. No one will ever trace it back to me. It will remain an unsolved affair before turning into a cold case. Your parents will cry for you, mourn for you." Kung took one step forward, stopping less than twenty inches from the door. "They will lay your body in the ground, where you can rot to feed the worms. And when enough years have gone by, every last soul in this city will have forgotten you ever existed."

Yukina's eyes were torn between defiance and the crushing realization that what he was saying was true. I raised my good hand. "Seeing as I'm booked in this room too, do I get all the same perks she does?"

Yukina tightened her jaw while Kung stared at me like I'd grown an extra head. "Joke if you wish, Mr. Vale, but I hardly need remind you that you are in as precarious a situation."

I smiled while I locked gazes with Kung. "Oh, I've been in a lot of those in my life... And I'm still here."

The round man hummed a little bit before he used his left hand to grip the cage door. While he pulled it open, both of the thugs with drawn weapons tightened their grip on their guns. My hopes sagged as I realized they were aware of us picking the lock and any sudden movement on our part would equal a bullet to the head.

So much for plan A.

Kung moved to the side, making room for us to walk out. "It is fortunate for you and Ms. Tsing that I prefer you both to be alive for the time being, Mr. Vale."

Neither one of us made a move to exit. "Why?" Yukina asked, suppressed anger leaking through her lips.

Kung shrugged. "If you'll kindly follow me to my office, I'll explain in details."

After glancing at his gunmen to make sure they had us covered, he waggled that fat finger at both of us to come out. Because I was closer and I had a better chance of surviving an extra bullet, I took the lead. I felt a gun barrel grind into the back of my neck before I was pulled to the side. I saw Yukina get the same treatment once she left the cell. Kung glanced at the rest of his men and waved a casual hand at the outer door. After letting the other three flunkies take the lead, he led us out of the room.

We followed Kung single file down a dimly lit concrete corridor. The gun stayed pressed into the back of my neck the entire way and it was very likely that Yukina was getting the same treatment. The whole place smelled like rotting cabbage, and my best guess was that we were in some kind of dank basement that connected to the sewer system. As we approached an intersection, I looked for a way to make a clean break.

Before we got to the actual intersection, my escort pulled me short. "Hold it."

I stopped in my tracks as two people turned into our corridor from the left, a young Japanese woman flanked by another of Kung's stooges. We waited while they walked by us, which gave me time to study her.

Dressed in a classic white kimono, she looked like a geisha. The impression was reinforced by her powdered white cheeks and the dark red lipstick on her mouth. She moved forward in small measured steps, her head held high underneath her strange coif, which seemed to be a headdress as white as the kimono. She passed by us without a word and without averting her gaze. I could make out the faint scent of an exotic flower lingering behind her, which killed off the cabbage smell for a second.

A bad feeling clutched the pit of my stomach. Everything about her posture and movements screamed, "lamb to the slaughter". What was a beautiful woman like that doing down in a horrible place like this? My fists clenched up but there was nothing I could do for her. So, instead, I turned to watch her go.

I noticed that her coif was even stranger from behind. It was like a sphere was placed on her shoulders. That thing was like a white fishbowl, but with a pizza-slice-shaped opening on the front. In fact, the whole thing reminded me of—

"Alright, let's move," the guard behind me snapped, driving in the gun for emphasis.

I got the hint and obeyed, the whole coif analogy flying right out of my head. Ah well...If it was important enough, it'd come back to me later. Assuming Lady McDeath wanted me to have a later.

———

Once we got to the end of the hallway, we entered another room to the right. This one was a lot fancier than the one we'd just vacated.

A thick emerald-green rug covered the floor, contrasting with the eggshell-white walls surrounding us. There was a large bookshelf that matched the oak desk in the rear left corner. Kung was sitting behind it, surrounded by his goons while he turned on the laptop sitting in front of him. All the goons had their pistols out, so my guard pulled his gun off my neck.

After typing a few keys, Kung turned the laptop around so we could see the screen. It was a black and white video— or a live security feed—of a small shop in Cold City's Little Japan neighborhood. *Mao's Herbal Teas and Remedies* was written in bold letters on the window pane. The sight made my blood run cold and I could see Yukina turning pale on my right.

Kung steepled his fingers beneath his heavy chin and studied us. "Interesting...While I have no solid ideas on what your actual relationship is to Ms. Tsing's uncle, Mr. Vale, the concern on your face tells me that it is far more than your usual client-contractor variety."

I was about to tell him where he could shove his threats when a thought hit me. That woman in the hallway—I finally figured what her coif made me think of...Pacman. Yup, her head looked like a tilted white version of the round open-mouthed eater of pellets. The thought made me smile.

"Is something about this situation amusing to you, Mr. Vale?" Kung asked his brow knitting closer together.

I kept the smile going and nodded. In my line of work, you learned not to look a gift horse in the mouth pretty darn quick. So if I had to resort to memories of silly 1980's video games to keep my morale up and the bad guys off-balance, so be it.

"What's this about?" Yukina cut in before I had a chance to follow up with a witty comeback.

Kung tapped the screen from behind with his pudgy pointer. "The man sitting next to this camera has a rocket launcher. He also has instructions to shoot this shop unless I call him every hour to ask that he postpone the deed."

"What do you want?" Yukina said, putting a little more volume in it this time.

Kung's round eyes narrowed to small dots as his smile grew. "Why, for you and Mr. Vale to restore the balance, of course, Ms. Tsing. I trust that I now have your undivided attention?"

2

LITTLE JAPAN

This whole week was simple enough. I had just wrapped up a very dull infidelity case by providing the necessary evidence to the client's lawyer at a café off from the courthouse. The way his eyes lit up on the photos and receipts I gave him, I knew both would play a pivotal role in the upcoming divorce case. The lawyer was nice enough to buy my breakfast as a small bonus, complete with an extra-large cup of green tea.

I'd just got back to my car when I got the call from Mad Mao. Now, if I'd known what the future had in store for me, I wouldn't have bothered picking up. But of course, I had no idea. I'd just been paid and he was a friend, so why not go along for the ride?

"Vale Investigations," I said, as I juggled to hold onto my car keys and my steaming cup of tea while holding my cell-phone to my ear with my shoulder.

A Japanese-accented voice greeted me on the other end

of the line. "Vale, this is Mao. I need to talk to you...In person."

I frowned. The old man sounded worried and, given the things he dealt in, it took a lot to make that happen. I glanced around and calculated that Little Japan was only three streets over. "No problem," I said into the receiver. "I'm in the neighborhood. Give me five and I'll be at your shop."

"*Arigato*," Mao said before ending the call.

I didn't take offense at the brief goodbye. It gave me a chance to open the door on my Corvette Stingray and get in. Although it was a sunny April Monday, the morning chill inspired me to run the engine for a minute.

Since most of the locals were at work by now, traffic was light and easy-peasy to merge with. It wasn't long before the Stingray was headed for Mao's shop. Once I got past the second block, the signs went from English to Japanese with the exception of the street signs.

Back in the mid-19th century, a lot of Japanese workers migrated here. At that point in our city's history, we were one of the busiest ports on the west coast, which made the fresh workforce always welcome, no matter its country of origin.

No one ever quite figured out why we got such a massive influx of Japanese, though. All we knew is they had set up shop in the same three streets wide, four streets long district around the northwestern part of town, a few miles north of the old docks. Over the next century and a half, it became the cluster of residential buildings, tiny specialized boutiques and restaurants it is today.

I parked the Corvette in front of the Emperor's Palace, its parking lot deserted except for employee cars. With its red and gold columned exterior that attempted to live up to its name, the place felt like your typical tourist trap. But I knew from personal experience that the food inside was better than average. Their blowfish, in particular, was something to die for. I made a mental note to get lunch there if all went well enough at Mao's.

I noted the closed sign hanging from the Palace's front door as I walked past it. Mao's boutique was near the next intersection. It was stuck in one of those setups typical for the area: a street-level shop with two floors of apartments above. The pastel-blue façade contrasted with the peeling yellow house on the left and the faded maroon one on the right.

I pushed open the front door of Mao's boutique, a chime announcing my arrival. A whirlwind of spicy scents launched a frontal assault on my nose, making me cough as my nostrils fought to get their bearings back. I knew from experience that it was a lost cause.

The boutique was small—six or seven square feet—with a wooden counter at the back. Behind the counter was a passage that led to some other rooms. Shelves lined every square inch of the walls, each one covered with round glass jars. Swear to God, or whoever's in charge, there must have been hundreds of them, all stacked in rows of tens or twelves, labeled with brown strips that had handwritten Japanese kanji on them. While I couldn't read the labels, I knew some of them were as harmful as medicinal plants and dried spices could be. But some of the others...Well, that was another story.

I tried breathing with my mouth, but wound up sneezing anyway.

"Bless you," a voice I recognized as the boutique's owner said ahead of me.

I looked around but couldn't see him. "Mao?"

As I took a step forward, a hand shot up from behind the counter and waved. "*Gomen nasai*, Vale, I'll be just an instant."

I heard the familiar *clink* sound of a glass jar being locked before Mao's head popped up behind the counter.

He was his usual self, his white, unruly hair hanging over his hard, aged face. Wrinkles marred his broad forehead, while his almond-shaped brown eyes danced wickedly within their sockets. He moved from behind the counter to stand in front of me.

Mao always dressed in white when he was working. Today, he'd added a dark-blue apron which told me he'd been prepping remedies in the back before I got here.

"You rang?" I asked, looking down at the shorter man. I'd never pulled out the measuring tape, but I guessed he was a little short of five feet tall.

"You never returned my amulet," he said, glaring up at me.

Even though I was six feet tall, his outraged face made me consider taking a step back. I ran a nervous hand over the back of my neck. "You know, funny you should ask. See, I sort of...lost it."

Mao's brown eyes narrowed, which made me swallow hard. The next words came spilling out of my mouth. "Long story short, I got into a fight with this Golem on the docks. Huge bastard, with a sour attitude, a little dry on the edges. Anyway, he was trying to kill me—"

"Big surprise," Mao interjected with a raised eyebrow.

"—and we were on the ground, you know, thrashing about. And there was this good-sized crack in the boards. I mean I know the city's broke, but they could make an effort—"

"This is your idea of 'long story short'?"

I held up my hand and took a deep breath to finish. "Well, bottom line is, it's sunken in the bay now." I sneezed again but got no 'bless you' this time.

Mao crossed his arms over his chest. His Japanese accent grew thicker than ever as he yelled, "You lost my amulet?"

"Hey, I survived the fight and killed the Golem, something I wouldn't have done without it. So...all's well that ends well?" I chanced a hopeful smile to go with that last statement.

Mao uncrossed his arms long enough to point an accusing finger at me. "You never bring my things back, Vale, never." He poked at my chest with his finger. "Do you have any idea how much time and material goes into making them? I should have you swim the bay until you get it back."

I held up both hands in a 'peace' gesture. "Look, I'm sorry, Mao," I said. "You know I am." And I meant every word of it. The short man had more than herbs and potions hidden in his boutique and his skills had saved my bacon on the streets more than once.

My friend was a Japanese Taoist sorcerer and practitioner of *Onmyōdō*, a traditional esoteric cosmology that was a mixture of natural science and occultism. It was a lost art, forbidden now in Japan, which is why it was only practiced in secret. And it was rarer in Occidental parts of the world like this.

Though the short, willowy man was eccentric—what

kind of guy lets himself be known by what was a girl's name in Japan?—he was good at his craft. The various trinkets, amulets, and potions he'd supplied over the years had yet to fail me. Too bad, as the old man pointed out, I failed him by not being able to bring them back.

"You called me here for something, Mao? Said we needed to talk?"

The finger stabbing stopped as a dark veil fell over the shorter man's eyes. He took two steps back to lean against the counter, his jaw muscles tightening. That told me all I needed to know about the seriousness of the situation. "How can I help?" I asked in a gentle tone.

Mao took a breath before answering me. "My brother, Pau Tsing, he owns a small boutique down the street. He's a swordsmith."

That was news to me. I'd no idea Mao had any family in America, but we'd never discussed our private lives before.

"Our family is a very ancient one," he went on, his eyes gaining a thousand-yard stare. "My ancestors made blades for the daimyo and the Imperial family until the Meiji Restoration. They were revered and rich. People who could afford it came from all over the islands to get a blade made by the Tsing clan. That precious skill was passed on down the generations to the eldest sons."

He sighed as his eyes shifted from the distant past to my shoes. "But, as they always do, times changed. It became harder to make a living that way. So my grandfather moved to America in the hopes of finding new customers, and—" Mao's mouth contorted as if he'd tasted something sour. "—and now Pau sells our blades to tourists."

His tone was so reproachful, I half expected him to spit on the floor to help make his point.

"I take it Pau is the eldest," I said.

Mao nodded. "Yes, by two years." He waved a hand to encompass the boutique. "As you can see, I chose another path."

I nodded, waiting for the rest.

"Though my brother and his wife tried, they have no sons. And I never married. So, in a few years, our name will die, taking the Tsing legacy with it."

Mao stopped talking, letting an awkward silence fall between us. His story was interesting, but I failed to see what it had to do with me or how my particular skill-set could help him here.

"Sorry about that," I said, more to break the silence than anything else.

My words seemed to bring him back out of his funk. "That's the way of the world, isn't it? Times change...and *everything* must come to an end."

I nodded, though I didn't like how he looked at me when he said it.

"My brother does have a daughter," he added. "Yukina."

I perked up. Now we were getting somewhere. "Something's happened to her?"

Mao sighed. "That's what I believe. She's been missing for several days, Vale. Her parents went to the police and forbade me from taking any actions of my own."

I raised an eyebrow.

"Though it's never been discussed, my brother has some idea of what I do and the circles you and I frequent. But you have to understand, Pau and his wife, they consider themselves to be Americans, which means they trust your system. Yukina's mother especially; she has so little consideration for my ancient ways."

While understandable, such a route sounded like a road to heartbreak. I trusted the system once too. It didn't give me anything but grief in the end.

"So you want me to have a discreet look around as a way to circumvent your citizen brother's wishes," I said.

Mao sighed again, shaking his head in dismay. "The moments you get direct, I find myself wishing you weren't. But yes, that's what I'm asking."

The pleading in his eyes decided my answer for me. "Sure, I can do that. Have the cops turned up anything yet?"

"No, and I doubt they will."

Mao's tone was so resolute that it made me frown. The local cops had their limits, but I'd never considered them totally incompetent on something as basic as a missing person case.

Catching my look, Mao added, "You don't know Little Japan like I do, Vale. It isn't what it used to be. There is a sickness growing on our streets. Our young, they all want to get rich fast. So they wind up selling drugs and weapons for easy money."

I shrugged. "Common enough story in any number of American neighborhoods, Mao. We both know that."

He reluctantly nodded. "True...It's just...I never thought I'd live to see it happen here too."

I got where he was coming from. Situations like that are always different when it happens on your home turf. "Why come to me with this?" I asked, still missing a piece. "You said yourself I don't know Little Japan as you do."

Mao's eyes went from sad to hard in the blink of an eye. "Because I know who you truly work for, Vale. And I also know, despite how you answer your phone, *investigations* are not all you do."

I shrugged again. "As many times as you've outfitted me, I guess you would know about my dealing with business from across the border."

Mao's nod this time was more firm. "I'll admit that being ignorant of how this district works could be a problem. But it also makes you a complete outsider, not beholden to any of the local power-players."

"You mean the gangs, right?" I asked, which got me another quick nod. "Okay, any idea if your niece got involved with them?"

The old man sighed again, absently rubbing his left cheek. "This, I do not know. Yukina…She has always had a temper. She was a sweet child, used to help me here at the shop. I tried to pass down some of my knowledge to her but she was far more interested in the ways of the sword. As she grew older, she saw all the inequalities and injustices this world had to offer and…"

Mao let his words hang in the air. I chanced a guess. "She tried to do something about it?"

"That's what I'm afraid of, yes." He returned behind his counter and sifted through a pile of paper. He pulled out a newspaper clipping and handed it out to me. "And frankly her timing couldn't have been worse."

I read the article title out loud. "Little Japan Vigilante Strikes Again."

In the middle of the article was a picture of a police car and two uniformed cops forcing a man with cuffs on into the back of it. The tagline below it read, *"The arsonist was arrested after the* fukushuu onna *left him chained by a fence outside his basement."*

"What's a fukchuchu—" Mangling that first word made me stop right there.

"Fukushuu onna," Mao corrected me, enunciating each word. "It means 'Avenging Woman'. She's a local vigilante that's been angering a lot of dangerous people in Little Japan. No one knows who she is, but tensions have been running high since she started going against the gangs."

Mao's eyes darkened some more, which made me feel for the shopkeeper.

"Yukina looks up to this woman," he added. "And I'm afraid this got her into trouble she can't get out of. Just as I said, she's a sweet girl, Vale, but these are turbulent times. All the gang lords are on edge and several women have gone missing already this year."

I frowned. "You think the two are connected?"

Mao's jaw tightened. "I don't know. Some had Yukina's temperament. Some, you never would have thought they'd swat a fly. But they're missing just the same. And now Yukina..."

The tears he'd been fighting back spilled down his cheeks. Brutal personal experience gave me a good idea of what he was going through...and what not to promise.

"I'll do my best to bring her home, Mao," I said. "On that, you have my word."

Mao wiped his cheeks and nodded, trying to make his lips form a hopeful smile. "If you can manage that much, some part of the Tsing legacy will get a few extra years."

3
RATTLE THE SNAKE

Information gathering is the first step in any investigation. That's why I asked Mao for all the details he could give me on his niece. Seeing as an introduction to her parents was off the table, I decided my next stop was going to be her apartment.

The nice thing about a closed-off neighborhood like Little Japan is that everything's within walking distance. I retraced my steps, going past the now-open Palace before turning into a parallel street that was a copy of the one I'd left. Per Mao's instructions, I was looking for a magenta house with a laundromat on the ground floor.

Of course, a simpler way to gather information would have been to call my source in the Cold City Police Department, but Sergeant Melanie Ramirez and I had once more hit the 'off' switch on our on-again-off-again relationship. Long story short, she'd been trying to get me to spill the beans regarding my off-the-books activities for years. Not long ago, she came close to getting all her questions answered. Incidentally, that also damn near condemned her to an hoary cliché of a fate worse than death.

The rules about mortals finding out about Alterum Mundum, home base of every mythic and legendary being that ever lived, are very strict and very simple. Rule Number One: "Don't tell anyone." Rule Number Two: "Don't even *think* about breaking Rule Number One."

So when an evil genie from across the border kidnapped Ramirez in the hopes of marrying her so he could use her essence as astral Powerade, it'd taken some A-level bullshitting on my part to keep her in the dark. Deep down, I knew it may have been one lie too many. As I dreaded to think this 'off' period we were in was how it was going to be, I found solace in the fact she was alive enough to hate me.

I found the laundromat easily enough. With the exception of some clothes in the washer, the place was deserted. After double-checking that initial observation, I climbed the stairs at the back of the waiting area. Yukina's flat was on the second floor, and Mao had supplied me with a key, which made getting in no hassle. The inside of the place was everything you'd expect from a twenty-one-year-old woman on a secretary's salary: small but cute, sparse but practical.

The kitchenette doubled as a living room while the bedroom acted as a study, dressing room and—going by the mic and machine in the corner—karaoke lounge. Cramped as it was, the apartment was neat and tidy. Nothing was left to chance when it came to organizing where everything went. Every nook and cranny was put to good use.

A casual glance around the place turned up nothing noteworthy. A few books on swordsmanship caught my eye but, given the family legacy, they were to be expected. Dust had gathered on some of the flat surfaces, but the plants in the kitchen window hadn't died yet. Both those clues corroborated Mao's estimate on the time of her disappearance being just a couple of days.

A picture in her bedroom had me pause for a moment. It was a family portrait, taken a few years back, I would guess. Looking at it, I discovered Mao's brother Pau was as short as he was. He stood on the left side of the portrait, dressed in dark trousers and a casual blue shirt. Pau's facial features were a little leaner than his brother's and his hair was cut short. Other than that, the siblings were remarkably alike.

On the other side of the picture stood Pau's wife, who had a few inches over her husband, even though she was wearing flats. She was thin and pale-skinned, dressed in a plain strapless number, her long black hair hiding most of her bare shoulders.

My quarry stood proudly between her parents, dressed in a white *karategi*, the traditional uniform used for karate practice and competition. A brown belt was neatly tied around her waist.

Yukina must have been fifteen or sixteen when the shot was taken. She had her father's height, her mother's hair and poise, and a wicked smile. It made me wonder what she was thinking when the picture was taken.

Placing the picture back on the shelf where I found it, I moved back to the living room to stand in the only empty corner this apartment had to offer. Forcing myself to relax, I took deep, measured breaths. Mao was right about me being more than a P.I. Being beholden to Death herself came with some unique benefits that helped with jobs like this. The one I was in the process of turning on—which I'd dubbed my "sixth sense"—was probably the most useful of the lot.

As my breathing slowed down, the world became clearer. It was as if someone had turned on the "high definition" setting in my eyeballs. Details were easier to make out, like the dip in the sofa which said Yukina had a habit of sitting with her legs folded to the left. The length difference of the carpet fibers showed me the path she liked to take to get from the sofa to the stove and back again—always on the right-hand side of the tiny coffee table in the center of the living room.

A few minutes later, I had to shut off my sixth sense and lean against a wall, breathing hard. Tapping into resources that weren't mine always came at a price, and this time was no exception. I was grateful it didn't cost me more than a few minutes of disorientation and weakness.

Though it hadn't turned up anything useful, that little experiment in perception enhancement gave me a better understanding of Yukina's personality. Discovering her routine, her motions and habits made me feel closer to her and allowed me to understand her personality. If I was going to retrace her steps, I was going to need to understand all the choices she made along the way. Every little scrap of insight helped.

I was about to leave when I heard the floorboards creak outside the flat. I froze, turning to face the front door. The letterbox at the bottom of the door squeaked as someone pushed envelopes through the slot. The floorboards creaked again and silence fell back over the place. The mailman was gone.

I went to the door and pushed the envelopes receptacle

open. There was about a week's worth of mail in there, mostly invoices with the occasional promotional leaflet thrown in. I was about to put them all back when I noticed the one thing that didn't add up. I did a double-take as I realized there were two electricity bills.

———

Naturally, one of those bills was for the apartment. But the second one was for a different address, about four miles south of Little Japan. I drove my car there, leaving it next to an aging gas station a block down from the mystery address. I was north of the old docks, an area more than ready for a date with the infamous Cold City wrecking ball. Everything around me was a mix of vacant warehouses and office spaces. The posted rates for rent were so cheap your first instinct would be to inquire about functional electrical grids and running water.

The address on the envelope led me to an ancient, worn-down building I couldn't believe was still standing. A glimpse at the letterboxes in the dingy lobby revealed there were only two tenants: an insurance company I'd never heard of on the fourth floor and a metallurgy workers' union on the third. The address on the envelope was for the second sublevel.

I was halfway to the stairs when a sound I recognized as a body landing hard against a garbage bin caught my ear. It was coming from out back. I changed direction from the stairs to the back door at the opposite end of the lobby.

The door opened up to a dead-end alleyway and a fight I rudely interrupted. A dark-clad silhouette turned to glare at my intrusion. The face was obscured by a dark red scarf which covered her mouth and most of her nose, but the short frame and lean body told me it was a woman giving me the stink-eye.

Next to her was a burly man in a dark three-piece suit down on all fours. A gun that must have belonged to him—a Glock by the look of it—was out of his reach. The sunglasses he was wearing were shattered on the left lens and blood was coming from his mouth in slow drops. The bin he was crouched next to had spilled half of its contents on the street, courtesy of the roughhousing.

Big this guy may have been, but he wasn't slow in the head. He took advantage of my timely distraction to lunge at the woman. I saw it happening before she did and tried to shout a warning.

I needn't have bothered. She raised both arms up to block him and took the opportunity to grab at one of his wrists. Using his own momentum against him, she sent him flying over her back and into the nearest wall in a matter of seconds.

The man landed with a loud cry and went down for the count. By the time I reached them, he was a moaning heap on the ground while the masked *femme fatale* had vanished around the left corner of the alley mouth. I kicked the gun further away from the thug's reach to be safe—no sense getting shot in the back—as my mind processed what had happened.

As a rule of thumb, I didn't believe in coincidences and I had the sinking feeling I knew who that fighter was. The Avenging Woman herself, and one of the only people in this town who might have the answers I was looking for. No choice for it, really; I leaped to the chase.

Four long strides took me out of the dead-end alley. Five more strides to the left and I caught sight of her again. She took another left turn, this time towards Collins Avenue, one of Cold City's major arteries. That fact alone made me force my legs to beat the pavement faster. If she got to the main road, it was a certainty that I'd lose her in the crowd.

I've always been good at running. It was a skill I acquired when I was little and later perfected when I joined the Navy. Damn if Uncle Sam wasn't big on PE for any and all branches of military service. No matter the weather, no matter the temperature, no matter the humidity, our superior officers had us running every single day we were on dry land. Our XO had a name for it: "Taking a ride on my personal highway to Hell". I swore once I got out, I'd never so much as jog again.

That's not the way it wound up working out. After I left the Navy, I kept the routine going for a couple of months. It was only after I readjusted to civilian life that I slacked off. I took days off and my running routine gradually morphed into a combination of jogging and swimming. That regimen allowed me to keep in shape without the need to wolf down proteins like I was Usain Bolt.

Today, I ran like the devil was after me and wondered if I should have trained a little harder. Fast as I was, the Avenging Woman's lithe body moved like the wind. I looked at her running and did some calculations in between breaths. Because I had longer legs, two of my strides equaled three of hers. So it didn't matter if she was faster than me right now; in the literal long run, I'd catch up with her.

That's when she reminded me there was more to any chase than speed. She took another sharp left into a parallel alley and disappeared from sight again. I cursed, pushing my legs harder while the adrenaline pumped fast in my veins. Not fifteen seconds later, I made the turn myself, zipping into that tiny corridor like a loose bullet. It took me longer than it should have to realize she was nowhere in sight. Took me longer still to stop running and reengage my brain.

Sweat beaded on my brow as I tried to locate my prey. The alley was only wide enough for a single car to pass through it and I sure hadn't heard any before I got there. Tall rows of residential buildings loomed above me on both sides. They were so high I knew sunshine had to be a rare treat, even on the brightest summer day.

A metallic creak had me turning around and looking up to locate the source. Silhouetted against the alley's darkness, I found my quarry. She was halfway through climbing up a service ladder, her hands grabbing the horizontal bars at a brisk pace.

I climbed after her as fast as my ragged breathing would let me. I put her at barely five feet tall, which made me smile. Since I was a foot taller, I had a longer reach. That meant once again I had an advantage that could let me catch up.

I expected to have to search for her again by the time I made it to the top. To my surprise, she was standing there on the flat rooftop, motionless while the clouded sun shined behind her back.

I studied her as I planted both feet on the flat surface. From the knee-high boots covering her slim-fit elastic jeans to the hooded leather coat shrouding her from head to toe, everything she wore was black. The only touch of color was the scarlet scarf over her face.

A gust of wind blew hard enough to make the sides of her coat part. That revealed the garment was cut in four long strips of leather, from hip to ankle, to allow for a wider range of motion. While this wasn't the kind of tactical gear I was used to seeing in combat, I could tell it was practical and offered decent protection without sacrificing agility. And it worked better than military camo when it came to mingling with a crowd.

Above the red cloth, two almond-shaped eyes glared darkly at me again. I raised both hands in a pacifying gesture. "I only—want to talk," I said between pants.

The pale white fingers of her right hand twitched as her eyes narrowed. I got past my panting to spit out my next words. "I don't know—who that guy was—and frankly, I don't care. It's not you I'm—I'm after. I'm looking for a—young woman."

I took a tentative step forward, which made her hand fly up to the sheathed blade she had strapped to her back. I took the hint and stayed put. "Please—I think she might be in danger."

"If she lives in Little Japan, she is." Her words were a reedy whisper that carried on the wind.

"I know," I said, nodding. "I heard about you. You're like me. You want to help these people however you—"

"We're nothing alike!" she cut in, fingers lacing around her weapon. She had it by her side, dark wooden sheath and all, an instant later. The sheath itself was long, thin and slightly curved. I knew only one blade shaped as such: the katana, Japan's sharpest and most famous sword.

I took stock of my own arsenal, which at this moment consisted of the short knife I had strapped to my right ankle. Seeing as I hadn't expected to fight Jackie Chan's long lost sister when I woke up this morning, I'd left my Sig Sauer pistol at home.

"Listen," I rose my hands up a little higher, palms still outstretched. "I don't want to fight you. I want to find my friend's niece."

The vigilante's answer was a war cry as she came at me with her sheathed weapon. She struck with the swiftness of a biting snake at my head. I brought my left hand up to parry while punching with my right to land a body blow.

She pivoted her chest out of the way in time to avoid my clumsy punch. I had no such luck with the knee she aimed at my gut. It caught me full strength in the solar plexus, knocking the wind out of me. I tried not to puke as the blow drove me to my knees. Another swirl of her torso later and her sheathed katana landed on the side of my head. My hands were too busy clutching my stomach to keep it from turning out my lights.

4

PRAYERS TO THE WIND

I returned to consciousness with a groan. Just breathing hurt and the steady cadence of raindrops wouldn't stop hitting me in the face. A quick glance around showed I was alone on the rooftop and drenched to the bone. Rolling onto my back, I reached a hand up to massage the tender spot that'd popped up on the side of my head. My fingertips found a large, sensitive lump and stroked it. That bright idea made me groan all over again from the pain.

"The hells have I got myself into this time?" I muttered while I went about the business of getting up on my unsteady feet. Once I was sure my legs would support my weight, I noticed night was starting to fall. The streetlights showed off a heavy rain washing down over Cold City with the street gutters near overflowing. Looks like it'd been doing this for most of the afternoon.

Going back down the service ladder was a lot slower than the climb up. Every rung I descended aggravated my bruised solar plexus. It made me grateful to get back on street level again, where walking didn't hurt so much.

By the time I reached Yukina's office building, my teeth were chattering from the wet and cold I was soaking up. Combine that with the pounding headache that came with the bump on my head, and it was enough to make me debate driving back to the Emperor's Palace, grabbing a meal to warm myself up and calling it a day. But leaving meant I'd have to come back later, which was a waste of time I wasn't prepared for. Not when a missing woman's life could be in as much danger as my attacker had implied.

I knew that armed thug who'd also dropped by—and was now long gone, leaving nothing behind but the shattered pieces of his sunglasses—could have been there for any number of reasons, most of which had nothing to do with my case. But I had made it a professional rule not to believe in coincidences.

The back door was still unlocked. Taking a look around the lobby, I found myself wondering if anybody bothered locking the front and back doors after hours. I shrugged off the question and made my much-delayed rendezvous with the staircase. I found myself fearing for Yukina's life as I took the steps down to the subbasement two at a time. If armed men were after her, Mao was right to call me in. Still, after the epic beating I'd taken, I wasn't sure if his brother and sister-in-law hadn't had more of the right idea.

I found the little office space Yukina rented. Its door was slightly ajar and not because she was lax on security. The chipping around the latch showed all the signs of being forced open with a crowbar. Her sparring partner made use of his free time once he got out of the alley—or maybe that was before I interrupted their fight.

After pulling the combat knife out of my boot and standing off to the side, I pushed the door open with my blade. I listened to the room for a couple of minutes before taking a step inside. When nobody attacked me, I took another one. The outside light let me make out the light switch on the left wall. Hoping all the water dripping off me wouldn't get me electrocuted, I turned it on.

Fluorescent lights flickered on from above. I noticed a couple of them were dead but the rest put out more than enough light to see by. Most of the space was repurposed into a martial arts dojo. A bamboo mat sat in the center. I could make out scuff marks on it which could only come from being trampled and stepped on repeatedly...Like, say, if you were training. A wooden weapons rack, showing off swords of various sizes, hung on the back wall like a warning sign. One slot in the middle that was the right size for a katana was noticeably empty. Hanging on either side of this were coats, pants, boots, and scarfs that were exact copies of what the vigilante was wearing.

Out of both respect and a desire not to leave any evidence, I went around the mat to get a closer look at the clothes. The lack of labels combined with exceptional craftsmanship that only comes from making such things by hand told me these were custom-made. I wondered if some of the people I talked to in my last big case could tell me more about that. Even so, the clothes being here told me all I needed to know. Yukina and the woman who'd knocked me out were one and the same.

I looked back at the wall where the light switch was and

saw something that didn't fit the dojo vibe: a massive cork-board filled with photos and slips of paper written in both English and Japanese. A few of the slips were below most of the photos, all of them of Asian men between the ages of eighteen and thirty. Some slips stood alone, marked with a question mark or a name. The higher up the chart, the older the men in them got, looking thirty or better, at a guess. At the top of this ragged pyramid was a photo of a heavyset man with fat oozing off his cheeks, marked by the name "Lao Kung".

Connecting these papers and photos were bits of yarn that were wound around the thumbtacks holding them up, making an inverted tree out of the whole mess. I'd been in enough police stations to recognize what I was looking at: a crime family organizational chart. To go to this much trouble meant our Avenging Woman had a serious hate on for this crew. Maybe they were the reason why she'd told me no young woman in Little Japan was safe? Backing up a little, I used my camera phone to snap some pictures of the chart.

Looking at the opposite wall, I spotted another corkboard that was the twin of the one I was standing next to. This too was dotted by paper strips and photos, but all of them were held in place by metal needles that gleamed in the light and no strings wove their way between them. Skirting the edge of the mat, I went over to this new board to take a better look.

The slips on this board were all handwritten. But unlike its sister board, a lot of different hands went into writing these notes. Some of them were in Japanese kanji that I'd need a translation guide to figure out. But a few of them were in English and every one was a desperate plea for help. A storekeeper asking for some muscle to keep the gang from taking "protection money" he needed to help his sick mother...A young boy who'd never walk again because of a stray bullet asking the *fukushuu onna* to give the ones who did it the same treatment...An elderly woman mourning the prostitute daughter who had always provided for her because some preening peacocks decided a whore's life was worth less than a dog's...I felt my anger spike a little higher as I read each note. Mao hadn't exaggerated when he told me a sickness was spreading within Little Japan. There were dozens of messages pinned to the board.

A photo stood in the center: the graduation picture of a smiling young Japanese woman. The note below it came from her mother, all but begging the Avenging Woman to return her child safely to her, by whatever means necessary.

I glanced at some of the other photos on that chart and the notes under them I couldn't read. How many of them had the same story to tell? How bad were things they had to turn to a self-made myth like Yukina to handle their situation? And how had all these notes found their way to the vigilante's lair?

Taking a deep breath, I remembered I still had my phone handy. I snapped a few shots of this corkboard too.

Once I was certain this place had given up all its secrets, I took a few minutes to wipe my prints off every flat surface I'd touched. It wasn't likely Yukina had a fingerprint kit handy or the cops were going to come by soon, but I knew a certain detective lieutenant who would dearly love for any excuse to bust me, so why give him any possible chance? I kept the handkerchief over my hand as I flipped off the switch and closed the door behind me.

The rain had stopped by the time I got back outside. I'd air-dried off enough in the building to not feel too chilly as I walked back to the car. As expected, nobody had bothered the Stingray while I was gone. The eye-catching speedster hadn't been my choice—it was a sort of a company car—but I needn't have been worried about local thieves. I don't know what mojo my boss had sprung on the car, but no one ever came close to it, no matter which shady neighborhood I parked in.

I made a point of turning the heater on to dry myself off the rest of the way back to the Emperor's Palace. After the day I'd had, blowfish sounded awfully tempting. My waiter, gods love him, was perceptive enough to see I'd been caught out in the rain and gave me some complimentary green tea to warm up.

After making a mental note to tip him extra for the consideration, I got back to thinking about what I found in the old office. I wondered if Mao had suspected Yukina was the Avenging Woman from the start. Strong sense of justice, the use of swords, thorough enough knowledge of the local gangs...A rookie beat cop could have drawn that line to Yukina in about two seconds. I remembered how much Mao kept emphasizing what a sweet girl she was back in the day. Maybe he never wanted to think of her as a vicious vigilante. That kind of willful ignorance happens to the families of addicts all the time. Still, why not share those suspicions with me? Why pull the damsel-in-distress card when he had to know I'd help her in any case?

That was something I chewed over until the blowfish

arrived. Best I could figure it was that the whole neighborhood had eyes and ears. Places like Little Japan could be more like small villages rather than parts of a city. Everybody had a tendency to know everybody else's business, so he may have been trying to protect Yukina from anyone who'd put her at the top of their shit list.

Speaking of shit lists, I took out my phone and pulled up the photo of the chart. I zoomed in on the pic at the top of the pyramid and frowned. Even with all this new info at my fingertips, I had no idea who Lao Kung was or where I could find him—and that was before we got into the other names below him.

I cursed as I put my phone away, alarming my returning waiter. I gave him a reassuring smile and said, "Sorry... Getting frustrated with some work stuff. You're doing fine."

He smiled in response and asked if I'd like some dessert. Being reasonably ahead on my cash for the moment, I told him yes.

As he walked away, I was forced to admit I wasn't familiar enough with the important players in Little Japan to even know where to begin on this case. This neighborhood had always been a little enclave beating to the rhythm of its own drum, a world away from the other parts of Cold City I knew. Mao may have thought that perspective would help me see this situation with fresh eyes, but that meant dick if I didn't know what I was looking at in the first place.

One dessert and a generous tip later, I was back on the streets, turning up my army-green jacket collar against the evening chill. I jogged back to the cozy warmth of the Stingray. I was planning on going home to grab a few hours of sleep, but the leads I found in the office kept tumbling through my head. Maybe the recent concussion I sustained had scrambled my thinking. Maybe the food in my belly had helped clear the cobwebs from my head. Either way, they say it takes one to know one.

Well, as luck would have it, I just happened to be on friendly terms with a mob boss or two.

5

INTIMATE CONVERSATION

R amon De Soto was, for all intents and purposes, what you would call a modern-day godfather. Officially, he and his wife Estella ran a popular-with-the-kids night-club called Smoke & Mirrors. And by popular, I meant you could be standing in line until daybreak unless you had an in with the right people. Of course, unofficially, this married pair was into a lot of other high-risk businesses this country has laws against, such as drugs, prostitution and a few other unsavory things I had the good sense never to ask about.

The De Sotos were everything you imagined South Americans to be: boisterous, suave, polite and extremely short-tempered if you put a foot out of line. But I'd done *El Jefe*, as Ramon was known to his men, a solid a few years back and he'd allowed me to live to tell the tale. Hells, he'd done me the honor of offering me a job, and the courtesy of letting me keep my head when I politely declined.

I never could shake the impression he didn't do either of those things with anybody. In fact, for reasons I never understood, he took a liking to me that manifested itself in the form of mutual favors and information. Even so, the danger I felt roll off him like heat waves made me avoid him unless I had a genuine need. But this case qualified as a "had to" situation.

As usual, I didn't bother with the line and went right up to the front door. My rundown attire was anything but appropriate for the club, so it was no surprise when the doorman put a hand the size of my chest in front of me.

"Back of the line, sir," he said in his deep bass voice, which let me know it wasn't a suggestion. I had a good idea his three-piece suit hid a handgun, just in case I was packing myself.

"I'm Bellamy Vale," I told him. "If he's got the time, I'd like to see *El Jefe.*"

Apparently, word filtered down the ranks about me since my last visit. The doorman dropped his hand into his pocket to fish out a flip phone. It looked like a plastic pebble inside his massive paw. "One moment, sir."

I nodded but I wasn't sure he saw it. He was too busy dialing someone. After a couple of seconds, he said into the receiver, "*Señora* De Soto, I've got a man here claiming to be Bellamy Vale."

After another couple of seconds, he relayed a detailed if unflattering description of my appearance. Then he nodded at the reply on the other end and said, "Right away, ma'am." Flipping the phone shut, he stepped aside and waved me in. "Wait for your escort once you get inside the door."

"When you said 'scruffy-looking', you meant in a cool Han Solo kind of way, yeah?" I asked as I stepped into the club.

Whatever answer the doorman came up with was lost on

me. The techno-music this place was known for was up to its usual eardrum-shattering volume, making me wince. I could make out the sea of sweaty, dancing bodies on the main floor, obscured by the dry-ice-generated smoke that hung like a thick fog over the place. The mirrors covering every inch of the walls gave the impression the place was a lot bigger than it was. The DJ, a woman whose only distinguishing feature was a half-shaved head, towered over all like a high priestess from the faux Aztec pyramid she was spinning her cuts from.

Well, almost all...I looked up to see a rather large booth looming over the whole scene, obscured by the smoke and one-way glass that kept anyone from looking in.

My escorts stepped out of the smoke, two more well-dressed human tanks that parted the kids around us like a prow parting the waters. The one on the left gestured at my arms, turned his palms up to the ceiling and raised his hands. I got the hint and held my arms out at a T-bone. Both men gave me a quick frisk. It didn't take them long to find my knife, which the one on the right put in his inside pocket without comment. We were done after that and the one on the left gestured towards the dance floor.

Three minutes of unbearably loud electronica later, we reached the back door of the dance floor, watched by yet another security guy. He opened it for us and promptly shut it once we stepped through. The noise from the DJ was instantly reduced to a distant throb, giving my ringing ears a chance to recover. In the meantime, we kept walking until we made it to a flight of stairs that took us towards the booth.

My escort on the right knocked on the door before opening it. A spacious office awaited us on the other side. The windows facing the dance floor were on the left, where a magnificent specimen of womanhood stood before them. Massive, defined muscles wound their way around her back, arms and legs, sheathed under light copper skin. Her powerful build was a match for her height, which came close to my own. No heels to enhance it, either; she wore stylish but functional flats. Her permed, curly hair, which was roughly the same color as her skin, was cut a little shorter than the last time I saw it. The dress she wore was a bit more upscale than what the clubbers below wore. It was a black, backless number which tightly clung to her well-muscled body, with prominent slits on either side that exposed her legs to the mid-thigh.

I only had a second to take all this in before Estella De Soto turned around to acknowledge our presence.

"*Gracias, señors,*" she said, the vowels richly pronounced. "*Sólo déjanos, por favor.*"

My escort nodded and the door closed behind me. Once it had, a smile that straddled the line between flirty and genuinely happy came over Estella De Soto's face.

"Bell, it has been far too long."

With four strides, she crossed the distance from the windows to the doorway and swept me up in a hug. As she followed that pleasantly strong embrace with a kiss on the cheek, I noticed the extra-large desk Ramon usually sat at was empty.

"Is Ramon around?" I asked.

She sighed as she let me go...mostly. She kept her hands on my shoulders and ran her left one down my chest with delicate strokes. "Alas, my dear husband is away on some important business. He will not return until close to the end of this month."

I couldn't hide my disappointment at this. "That's a shame. I was hoping he could help me tonight."

The roving hand settled on my breastbone and massaged it gently. "I share your disappointment, Bell. I have been so very, very lonely without him."

The look she was throwing my way worried me. She'd never made any secret of being just as fond—or, gods help me, even more fond—of me as her husband. And yes, I was as drawn to her as any straight man with a secure enough ego to not be intimidated by this woman's powerful physique could be. But the last thing I wanted to do was act on that. Sleeping with another man's wife was a bad idea. Sleeping with the wife of Ramon De Soto was a suicide wish.

"Even so," she continued, her hand stroking my chest with a gentleness that belied her size. "I would hate for you to have come all this way only to leave empty-handed. Are you certain there is nothing I can do for you in my husband's absence?"

Swallowing hard, I managed to choke out, "I need help on a case...The kind of help only you and Ramon could give me."

She pouted at my answer while her strokes intensified. "Oh, and how could I possibly help with that? I am merely Ramon's loving wife and thus lack the true knowledge of certain things that is his birthright."

That honeyed half-truth was enough to shatter the lust spell she was weaving over me. "A loving wife who happens to run the day-to-day operations of her husband's business," I said with narrowed eyes and a sly smile. "That would be why he left you in charge while he's gone, right?"

Estella dropped the flirty attitude, right down to the

stroking hand which fell back by her side. Her smile became appreciative before she burst into a loud, amused laugh. Laughter was the least pleasant sound either De Soto could make, as it always seemed to imply they were going to kill you when they were done. But instead of that, Estella swept me up in another hug and pressed a kiss into my forehead so hard I wondered if I had just acquired a new tattoo there.

"*Muy bueno, pero muy misterioso,*" Estella said, pulling her hands away this time. "Ramon did say you had extraordinary focus when you were engaged in your work. While I would never doubt my husband's word, I had to see for myself. Come...Sit."

I made a beeline for the nearest chair in front of the desk while Estella took her own place behind it. Once we were both settled, she said, "I heard you and Sergeant Ramirez are no longer seeing each other. Has there been a misunderstanding between you?"

My eyebrows rose in surprise. The smile she gave me was gentle, almost motherly. "Both Ramon and I like to stay informed of persons whom we consider assets. And it certainly includes any romantic arrangements said assets may have."

"Neither of you had a problem with me seeing a cop, did you?" I asked, as afraid for myself as I was for Ramirez.

She waved away my concern. "Oh no, far from it. You know our own love story has been far from conventional. As such, we do not judge that of others so long as they are not an impediment to our business."

"Which, I'm hoping, we never were?"

"At all," Estella confirmed with a nod. "But you did not come out all this way to gossip with me about your love life.

Tell me everything you can about this case and I shall give you a truth for a truth."

Seeing no reason to hold back, I gave Estella what she asked for. I only had a day's worth of investigation to recap, so it didn't take me too long. I did notice Estella perk up when I mentioned the mother's note about her daughter. While Ramon had never told me about the part of the world he and his wife had escaped from, I knew it was anything but genteel. There was a better than even chance they'd seen similar things happen along the way.

Once I finished, Estella leaned back in her chair in deep thought. I decided to follow her example and waited. She broke the minute of silence by saying, "You will understand the information I can give you is, by its nature, limited, *si*?"

I shrugged. "Anything you can tell me that I don't know is more than I had before."

She nodded and continued. "By mutual agreement with the local organizations, we have largely stayed out of Little Japan. Of course, there are some trading of goods, the odd exchange of information and the occasional alliance to discourage outsiders from establishing a foothold in our respective territories."

I nodded in understanding. "But by and large, you make a point of getting out of each other's way."

"*Si* and thus both sides have prospered. I know Ramon has a personal distaste for Lao Kung and the rest of his men."

"I'm guessing he does a good job hiding that distaste when he and Kung have to talk?"

Estella gave the windows behind me a thousand-yard stare. "Mercifully, it is not often or we would have long since erupted into a war, I fear. I must admit Lao has certain qualities which mirror my husband's own: a solid work ethic, a commitment to neatness and cleanliness, and a word that can be trusted in all things, be they deals or threats."

"Sounds like you admire him," I noted, tapping the chair arm with my own finger.

She broke off her stare to look at me and shake her head. "It is more of a professional appreciation than anything else. I would hardly be the correct choice to run Ramon's daily operations if I failed to acknowledge my potential ally or opponent's strengths."

"But Kung *is* the dominant power in Little Japan right now?"

"Very much so," Estella confirmed, rising to her feet. "All others who have operated within his sphere of influence have flocked to his banner or been buried in places that have no grave markers."

I made to rise myself but Estella held out her hand. "No...sit."

While she came around the desk, I listened for the sound of quiet footsteps. The last time I'd been in this room, local mob boss Alonzo Vittorini sat in this chair and hadn't heard the knifemen coming for him.

"You have to understand something, Bell," she said, stopping in front of me. "Whatever Ramon's opinions of Lao are, both of them have an interest in keeping order within our unique ecosystem. This is why we have our respective associates stay away from each other."

"Just the same, I imagine you both keep an eye on each other," I suggested. "How can you be sure order is being kept otherwise?"

"Of course," she said, walking off to the right of my chair.

"However, there is a great deal of difference between being watchful and disrupting the status quo. We both know the latter is practically your trademark."

I grew nervous as she walked out of sight. "Look, I never want to make the kind of messes I—"

"And I believe you," Estella assured me while sliding both her hands from my shoulders to my chest again. "I do. But...you have a habit of leaving a great deal of destruction in your wake, Bellamy Vale. That is far too risky. You could well start a war we are not prepared to win."

I licked my lips. If I didn't do something fast, there was an excellent chance I'd be as dead as Vito in a few seconds. Hoping my detective senses were accurate, I said to her, "What about the girls?"

Estella's hands drew back slightly. "Come again?"

"The girl whose mother is desperate to find her and Mao's niece who was doing her damnedest to find her...They don't want a war either."

The hand on my right shoulder came off but the one on the left traced its way back up to my collarbone. "The chart you found in that subbasement begs to differ on your latter point."

"Even so," I persisted, watching Estella step back around and her hand fall away again, "both of them have families who want nothing to do with neither yours nor Kung's business. Both of them want to know their loved ones are okay. One word from you—the right word—and you may be sparing those families a lot of pain."

"And the niece?"

"I can't promise anything, but I can do my best to talk some sense into her."

She was standing right in front of me again. The deep breath and subsequent sigh she let out told me I hit the right button. She looked reluctant but what I'd told her was something she couldn't ignore.

"Very well, Bell," she said, looking down at me. "But it will cost you."

That wasn't a surprise. When it came to the De Sotos, you always paid for any favors they did you. "Name your price," I answered with a shrug.

The sweet and feral smile she gave me was so bright I wondered if I'd made a mistake. "A favor...One that is to be collected at a time and place of my choosing."

Her face darkened as she leaned down, which also gave me a profound look at her cleavage. "And this favor applies only to me. Ramon is to never know of it or hear of it. Do I make myself clear?"

I swallowed thickly. "Crystal."

She smiled again, grabbed my arms and pulled me back to my feet. I came up so fast I fell into her chest before I found my footing.

"There is one warehouse where we know Lao conducts his unofficial business," she said, paying my stumble no mind. "You will find it at 2518 Northam Street, near the old docks."

She gently but firmly steered me towards the door. A shadow of sadness crossed her face when we got there. "Even with the speed you have been applying to your investigation, I fear you may be too late. Sadly, many old traditions have deep roots in such insular cultures, and your friend's niece is but of the right age for that."

I wanted to ask her more about that but the look on her

face told me this interview was over. That was confirmed by the words she spoke, accompanied by a final hug and kiss. *"Cuídate, mi amigo."*

A minute later, I was being led out the back of the club by my escorts, who'd been hanging close to the office door. My knife was handed back to me before the door closed. As soon as it shut, I stuffed it in my jacket pocket and made a dead run for the Corvette. If time was as short as Estella implied, I needed to get to that warehouse ASAP.

6

FULL CIRCLE

The first three blocks I drove were as clogged as Times Square on New Year's Eve. It wasn't solely because of Smoke & Mirrors; the whole area was packed with clubs jostling for attention and customers crowded them on any given night. All that made the going slow until I got past the traffic lights at Park and Snyder. After that, the traffic was a typical Cold City weeknight, so light you might as well be the only person on the road.

It took me so much time to get out of the area that I almost didn't want to stop by my apartment to pick up my Sig. However, my place was on the way and going in less than well-armed sounded like a sure way to get over-whelmed. So I took the time to run in, grab my P226 and two spare 9mm magazines before I double-timed it to the warehouse.

After confirming the address via the GPS on my smart-phone, I drove past it. Northam Street was a little closer to my usual stomping grounds than Little Japan; that's how I knew about the abandoned loading dock around the corner on Fairweather Avenue. I parked my car in the shadows, which swallowed it whole. That gave me all the cover I needed to slip out of the driver's side door. As always, I left the keys in the ignition in case I needed to make a hasty exit. Closing the door as quietly as I could, I stayed low to the ground and walked towards the warehouse.

The entire six blocks around me were nothing but warehouses. They were of 1990s vintage, with a few odd 21st-century specimens. Many businesses here went under when the old docks dried up, while others were put on the market as a result of the Great Recession. Still, enough of them stayed in business to make this area semi-functional and a lot of the abandoned ones were repurposed. For instance, I knew of one that was used as temporary housing when our former mayor bombed six city blocks to bring about the end of the world about half a year ago. Another one became one of the most secure storage units in the city, trusted by citizens and criminals alike. Police presence wasn't unknown here, but it was pretty thin on the ground during evening hours. It'd take a ruckus like what the ex-mayor pulled to get them out here this late.

Though I shut off the GPS on my phone, finding the right warehouse wasn't hard. It was the only building on the block with the lights on. I slipped down the nearest alley to it and crept towards the back. Once I got there, I peeked around the corner for guards. After five minutes of no footsteps or patrols, I concluded that all the security was on the inside.

That left me with the problem of how I was going to get in. As I looked up, I noticed one of the upper windows was open. A quick glance showed none of its neighbors were. I also took note of how close the open one was to a drain pipe on the corner that ran close to the building's right side. Putting it all together only meant one thing: Yukina. She was already inside and causing who knows how much impulsive trouble in the process.

If the man who visited her lair this afternoon was one of Kung's men, and I was pretty certain he was—as I said, I don't do coincidences—then the Avenging Woman's true identity wasn't much of a secret anymore. Whatever plan she was working on, the earlier intrusion forced her into action.

However brief our encounter on that rooftop was, I got the feeling Yukina wasn't the type who liked to play it safe and build a good defense as she waited for the enemy to attack. No, she struck me more as the shoot-first-patch-wounds-later variety.

I sighed and rubbed my face. I didn't see any better way to get inside without attracting attention. So, despite being less agile, weighing a lot more and not being dressed for the occasion, I'd have to do it the way Yukina had.

I ran up to the warehouse and flattened myself against the wall. I took another minute to listen for any guards who might be on the prowl upstairs. All was quiet so I got on with it.

The pipe turned out to be a lot sturdier than it seemed. The metal braces holding it up were the right height and strength to be good hand- and footholds. When I got to the window itself, I grew nervous. While my anti-death insurance would—probably—keep me from lethal harm, I was high enough to break a limb if I slipped. *So don't slip, genius,* I chided myself as I went up one more brace.

The window opened inward, which made getting inside a lot easier than it would otherwise have been. Still, my landing was noisy, making me do a quick scan of my surroundings, weapon in hand. I was on a metal balcony, roughly the same height as the hooded overhead lights that lit up the place. Down below, it looked like a typical warehouse with its pallets of shrink-wrapped goods filling out the shelves. All that clutter left a few spacious corridors you could drive a forklift down, but it also left a lot of narrow passages only a person could squeeze through. Going by the maze of catwalks around me, this was the level you wanted to be on to stay safe and keep an eye out for trouble.

I spotted my first dead body on the left catwalk, way too big to be Yukina. I did another low walk over to take a look. As I expected, this blank-staring corpse was killed by a blade, his throat cut from ear to ear in a jagged stroke. I noticed his right forearm was sliced to the palm, which explained the gun that was four inches from the hand and two inches from the catwalk edge. Figuring some extra firepower wouldn't hurt, I grabbed the dead man's weapon, stuffed it in the waistband at the small of my back and kept going.

I heard voices on the other side of the warehouse. While I couldn't make out the words, the diction and accent sounded Japanese. The catwalk I was on turned sharply to the left before opening towards a lit office area. I could make out a door on the opposite side of the office through the window. It had a fresh coat of red sprayed on it that resembled a slash. Subtle, Yukina was not.

I found myself grateful the door handle didn't have any of the slowly-drying blood on it. I was less grateful to see another dead guard blocking up the entrance like the world's grisliest doorstop. I stepped over him, slid through the space and closed the door behind me. The guard had a buddy off in the corner, staring forever at the crimson pool that'd come out of his punctured stomach.

I had a hard time reconciling the body count with the picture of the grinning teen I saw in Yukina's flat. I dreaded to think what could be responsible for the birth of such a cold-blooded vigilante persona.

On the wall over the corpse were enough pictures of young women to cover every inch. They had small white labels attached to each one, all written in Japanese. I crawled over to it and stared for a minute. After a while, I noticed a pattern to the pictures. They were all Asian, likely Japanese, somewhere in their 20s, thin with pretty features. I was taking all this in when I stopped at one in particular...The picture of the missing girl I saw on Yukina's wall.

"What in all the hells have you got yourself into this time?" I muttered through gritted teeth. The way these pictures were aligned and neatly labeled made me uneasy. It was like I was staring at a catalog of some kind.

A cell phone buzzing shook me out of my contemplation: the dead man's by the door. It buzzed about three more times before it stopped.

"Not good," I whispered, making a grab for the knife in my boot. It wouldn't be long before somebody came to check on the guards. Time to get scarce.

A peek outside showed the rest of the way was clear. In the distance, the voices I heard earlier were still going. I slid out the door and kept walking low towards the noise.

The voices grew more and more distinct the closer I got. Of course, since the entire conversation was in Japanese, that didn't do me a hell of a lot of good. I noted the catwalks remained clear as I rounded the last shelf of pallets to see the source of the voices. The lights in the immediate vicinity were a little too close and bright for my liking. As I searched for a safer position, I noticed some prominent shadows around the windows ahead, cast by some of the shelves. They wouldn't ward off a flashlight beam but they'd get me out of sight. I made a beeline to the nearest one and kept watching.

Lao Kung was heavier than his picture made him out to be. He made me think of Sidney Greenstreet in *The Maltese Falcon*, suavely trying to persuade Bogie to throw in with him. The men around him were a lot more fit and wore flashy street clothes that all but screamed "gang" to me, except for the two that stood just behind Kung. From up here, the three-piece suits they wore did little to hide the bulge of the handguns they wore at their sides. The bodyguards stood tensed, clearly on the lookout for trouble, but none of them ever bothered to look up.

The rest of the party stood around three statues that looked like they were freshly unpacked from the dismantled crates around them. I couldn't make out too many details on them, thanks to the glare from the lights. It seemed they were fifteen inches tall and of the animal kingdom variety. A turtle, a dragon and a big bird, if I was not mistaken. The reflective white hue on each of them told me they were most likely made from marble, but the finer details eluded me.

A heavy garage door opened underneath me, blasting my ears as badly as the music at Smoke & Mirrors had, and rattling the iron structure beneath my feet.

When the door clicked into place, the distinctive sound

of a woman's high heels headed towards Kung and his people. From what I could see through the grill of the catwalk, the new arrival was a Japanese woman of medium height. The overhead lights caught her blonde hair dye and the blue-black power suit she wore. I caught a whiff of authority and command about her and could tell from her walk she was pissed.

Kung gave her a deep bow, accompanied by what had to be a Japanese greeting.

I rolled my eyes. Was I going to need subtitles for this entire conversation?

"Unless you have the fourth statue somewhere other than here," the woman snapped in Japanese-accented English. "I fail to see what is so good about this evening, Mr. Kung."

I did my best to repress my sigh of relief. At least now I wouldn't have to deduce what was going on strictly through their body language.

"My expert," she said, coldly motioning to the man who'd come in behind her heels. He was broad-shouldered and dark-skinned, and I gathered the switch to English was made for his benefit. Without waiting for further invitation, he made his way to the statues, crouching down by each one in turn.

"I am certain you will find them satisfactory," Kung said in an oily tone.

The blonde woman turned an icy cold stare at him. "For your sake, they better be."

She stood motionless, surrounded by her four body-guards, as everyone waited for the inspection to be over.

The African-American man eventually stood up, readjusting the glasses on his nose as he did so. "They are, Miss. Intact and genuine, all three of them." There was a certain reverence to his words, revealing the high value of the pieces he'd just inspected.

"As agreed," Kung said, bristling a little.

"Do not flatter yourself, Kung," the woman said, walking past him to look at the statues. "Satisfactory these may be, but to date, *you* have been anything but."

From the way Kung was holding up his hands in a placating manner, he didn't think he was either. I happened to glance at one of the shadows further down and thought I saw something move.

While I was puzzling that out, Kung said, "Surely you can see the situation could be far worse. And we know where the final statue resides."

"I am paying you a small fortune for said statue to stand alongside the others," the woman replied, unimpressed with his explanation. I, on the other hand, was looking at something far more impressive: the shadows revealing the shape of Yukina in her full Avenging Woman gear, complete with the red scarf obscuring the lower half of her face.

"And that particular feat *will* be accomplished shortly, I promise," Kung answered, using his nervousness to help sell his sincerity.

Yukina carefully slipped out of the shadows to come closer to the catwalk's edge. I heard a disgusted grunt from the woman below that made me look at her again. She was handing the fat man three bound stacks of hundred dollar bills. Kung reached for them and the woman tightened her grip.

"We both know this set is useless without all of its

pieces," she reminded him. "As such, you have three days to make good on your word. Should you fail, you will not welcome my return."

Letting go of the money, she spun on her stylish heel and marched right back out the door she'd come through. Her minions were quick to gather the statues and follow their mistress out. I thought I saw Kung's hand shake a little as he put the money away.

I glanced over at Yukina to check on her only to find a guard she hadn't killed right behind her. He was raising his hand to strike her with what looked like a blackjack.

I yanked out my Sig, leapt to my feet and yelled, "No!"

It was all for nothing. I'd barely got the word out when the sneaky thug knocked Yukina out cold. As a consolation prize, I drew the attention of the guys down below. Before I could aim the Sig that way, one of them pointed his gun at me and fired.

I felt a white-hot needle lance its way through my shoulder, spinning me around. It made me trip over my own feet and sent my head crashing into the catwalk guardrail. I was out cold in seconds.

When I woke up, I was sharing a cell with Yukina and all our weapons were gone.

———

Yukina and I stared at Mad Mao's shop through the CCTV in Kung's office.

"If my attention were any more focused, you'd be dead," Yukina said, finally answering the gang lord's question. Reckless methods aside, I had to admire this young woman's strength. Outnumbered, outgunned and yet her voice was as strong as the steel her katana was forged from.

Kung let his lips stretch into a smirk. "And what say you, Mr. Vale? Can I assume you too have no distractions that would take your mind off the moment at hand?"

"Believe it, fat man," I said, letting my impotent anger leak into my voice. "Now, are you going to tell us what you want or do we keep guessing?"

Kung leaned back in his chair, pursing his lips in thought. "To save everyone time and potential misunderstandings, I have to ask this...How much of my meeting with my buyer did you see?"

I could see tears mingling with the hate in Yukina's eyes as she said, "I came after you had unpacked the statues, but before you groveled before that woman like the dog you are."

A flash of anger flashed across Kung's own face, prompting me to interject, "That's about as much as I saw too. Sounds like you've got yourself one unhappy customer, Kung."

The mob boss of Little Japan rose from his seat, his eyes still smoldering with anger. "You have a remarkable gift for understatement, Mr. Vale. Being short one of those statues carries severe penalties I dare not contemplate."

"And yet she paid you your money," Yukina noted.

"Half of my money, Ms. Tsing," Kung corrected her. "It was both an acknowledgment of what I had accomplished thus far and a warning I should finish what I have begun. While I am not the sort of person who walks out on a deal, walking away from this one is not a viable option."

"Which is where we come in," I deduced. "We'll be the ones grabbing that last statue in the set."

"Correct, Mr. Vale," Kung acknowledged, reaching for a manila folder sitting on the right side of his desk.

He pushed the folder forward before turning the laptop back around. When it became obvious neither I nor Yukina was going to make a grab for it, Kung flipped it open. The top page displayed the familiar crest of Cold City's Historical Museum. Kung flipped it back to reveal a color photo of the final statue, a rampant tiger made of marble. It was encased in a clear display box with a gold nameplate obscured by the camera flash.

He looked between the two of us. "You both have approximately forty-eight hours from the moment you leave this establishment to give me this final piece. Otherwise, Ms. Tsing's uncle is a dead man."

7

STRATEGY SESSION

The killer sales pitch concluded, one of Kung's goons gave me the folder before another one slapped a blindfold over my eyes.

"You *do* want us to read this, right?" I grumbled, holding up the folder for emphasis. The only answer I got was a gun poking my ribs again and a hand turning me around for what I guessed was the exit. I figured Yukina was getting the same treatment.

After that, we were pushed back into the corridors. This time, we made a lot more twists and turns as we walked. Even without the blindfold, I doubt I could have found Kung's office again without a mil-grade GPS tracker to help me out.

The guard's hand pulled me back, bringing me to a halt. The blindfold was pulled off right after that. The nearest electric bulb glinted off the ladder right in front of us. I spotted a slightly open manhole cover at the top. Behind me, Yukina snapped out a question in Japanese angry enough to make me glance over my shoulder in concern. I saw her guard answer it and point up to the cover. Yukina flared her nostrils but looked away.

After sticking the folder in an inside pocket of my jacket, I made my way up the rungs. This was way easier after the drain pipe I climbed earlier, even with the sore shoulder reminding me of recent injuries. The cover was easy enough to move aside and once I had, I crawled back to the surface. Yukina was a couple of seconds behind me. Once she was clear, something flew up the open hole before landing at our feet. I scrambled backwards until I realize it was my Sig. My knife came next, followed by Yukina's sheathed katana. Looking horrified that her weapon was thrown like a stick, she yelled more fast and furious Japanese down at our now-ex-captors. The yelling echoed off the nearby walls and made me worry about attracting trouble.

"Some people have no respect for quality," I quipped, hoping to lighten the mood a bit.

She gave me a snarling growl for that crack. I got the hint and decided to retrieve my weapons in silence. As I did so, I got a better feel for our new surroundings. We were in an alley three buildings down from Kung's warehouse; we were in a dead-end. I spotted Fairweather Avenue outside the alley mouth.

"I don't suppose you have a car nearby?" Yukina asked, picking up her sword and unsheathing it to check for flaws.

My own weapons securely stowed, I answered, "As a matter of fact..."

I pointed towards the street. She pulled out her blade the rest of the way and gave it a quick but thorough inspection with her fingers and eyes. Once she was satisfied, she sheathed it and we walked. Despite the head start I had, she was by my side in seconds and she had no trouble keeping up with me.

The next alley on the right served as a decent shortcut to the loading dock. Yukina's eyes widened and then narrowed at the sight of my fancy Stingray. "Well, this is nice and inconspicuous."

I sighed and held up my hands. "I know, I know, it sticks out like the proverbial sore thumb. It's not mine."

"Then whose is it? And why would someone give you this?"

I chuckled, reaching for the door, "Someone you never want to meet, and 'give' is a very generous term."

To her credit, Yukina didn't say anything else before we got in. She made a point of stowing her sword in the back seat, the hilt carefully placed so she could pull it at a moment's notice. I hoped she didn't have to do that on the drive over. Aiming the car towards Fairweather, I heard her take in a sharp breath. "You've been injured."

"Caught a bullet back at the warehouse," I told her. "Just a flesh wound...Should be fine with enough TLC."

When she didn't say anything else, I figured my explanation was accepted. That detail taken care of, I dialed the one person in my contacts list who could help us. After putting my cell on speakerphone, I laid it in my lap so I could focus on driving. Not that this was a challenge on this near-empty road, but still...

In place of a hello, I got a cut-glass British accent. "Bell, what in Tartarus are you doing ringing me up directly?"

I knew I was breaking my friend's new contact protocol the moment I hit dial, but there was no time to jump through ten hoops to get help. "You know I wouldn't do it if it wasn't important, Zian," I answered.

"Oh, it bloody always is with you. The usual spot, fifteen minutes?"

"Works for me...See you soon."

I heard the distinctive chime of the phone hanging up. Yukina asked me, "Protocol?"

I shook my head, "Yeah, I'm not supposed to call him directly. There's this web address I'm supposed to go to in order to get a code, and then I have to send it to an encrypted email address. And wait for a callback from a secure line."

She frowned at me, "Is he a cop or part of another gang?"

I shook my head, letting a knowing chuckle bubble up my throat. "Zian? Neither. His dad is a very important power player and Zian does everything he can to avoid his old man's wrath."

"And doing you the occasional favor tends to provoke that wrath?"

I didn't know how to answer, but I gave it my best shot. "Depends on what I'm doing and how generous Zian's dad's feeling that day."

Yukina's face got thoughtful. "So why risk getting in contact at all?"

"Because this job is going to require more than our collective skill-set. Doing a B&E on the Historical Museum means dealing with a top of the line security system. That's where Zian comes in."

Yukina nodded and leaned her head back in the seat. "Well, tonight proved how much we both suck at making a clean getaway. A little extra help certainly wouldn't hurt."

The car rolled to a stop at a red light. There wasn't

anybody else at this intersection but Cold City had installed cams in all their traffic lights. The last thing I needed was a traffic ticket and the extra attention from the CCPD that might bring.

While watching the light, I asked my passenger, "So how did you find the warehouse?"

"All his men know of it." Yukina's lips curled in remembrance. "I beat it out of one of them a few weeks ago."

"And yet you waited until tonight to make your move," I said, testing the waters. "Were you interested in those statues? Or the woman buying them?"

"Ms. Wada is of no concern to me," she said, her smile turning sour. "Kung knows my identity now. The plan was to get him before he got me. I didn't know the sell was going to happen tonight and the warehouse was going to be packed with extra security."

As I guessed, the altercation I interrupted earlier had set tonight's events into motion. Yukina was in a precarious situation long before we got roped into working for Kung, and her clenched jaw told me she knew that as well as I did. As for getting herself out of it, well...

"Ms. Wada. That's what the peroxide blonde goes by?" I asked, offering her a change of focus. After seeing Yukina's nod out of the corner of my eye, I continued, "What's her story?"

"What little I know of it doesn't add up to anything good," Yukina admitted as the light turned green. "She's from some old and powerful family back in Japan, and has been doing business with Kung for the last three months."

Tapping the accelerator, I asked, "Was it all just to get those four statues?"

"As far as I can tell, yes. That is the sole reason she came to America. From what my source could tell me, she had never left Osaka before."

"'Source'," I echoed.

She continued as though she hadn't heard me. "Though why the number three of one of Japan's largest banks would be interested in those statues eludes me. And why did she bother coming here herself?"

I decided to let my earlier question go unanswered, and changed my line of questioning. "Do you know where Kung..." I struggled to find the right word, "...*purchased* the three he already has?"

"They were liberated from their rightful owners all over the globe. Two were shipped from Europe and the turtle was stolen from some rich guy's penthouse in LA last week." Yukina sighed as the buildings outside zipped by. "Seems like we now know how they intend to get their hands on the last one."

I took a turn in a quieter street and remained tight-lipped as I mentally lined up everything I knew. It would seem Yukina and I had a lot in common. If things were different, she would have made a good P.I.

Two turns later, I realized something didn't add up.

"Wada and her statues is just something you heard about on the way, wasn't it?" I asked. "You were pursuing another line of enquiry, initially. What was it?"

"You're a lot smarter than my uncle made you out to be," she said, sidestepping my question.

It was my turn to look surprised. "He told you about me?"

"Not specifically," she clarified while the buildings on

the right gave way to the coastline. "But he did talk about this *gaijin* who uses his...other services regularly. One of his favorite complaints is 'how good of a detective can he be if he keeps losing what I give him?'"

I chuckled. "Yeah, sounds like something he'd say about me."

A smile tried popping up on Yukina's face but it crumbled away as fast as it sprang. It didn't take as good a detective as me to know she was thinking about Mao's safety. Best to distract her.

"Back at that office on the catwalks," I said. "I saw the wall of photos, the one with all those women."

Yukina's face hardened at my statement. "That wall is why I was there."

Parts of our brief rooftop encounter came back to mind. "Is that photo album what made you say no young woman in Little Japan is safe?"

Yukina found the coastline a lot more fascinating to look at than the road ahead. When the answer came, her voice was subdued. "That wasn't a photo album, Mr. Vale. That was a menu."

I frowned at the asphalt ahead of us. "A menu?"

She sighed. "When tourists come by the Emperor's Palace, the owners don't bother translating the meals to them. They give customers pictures to look at instead, so they can point at what they like and it saves everyone time and headaches. The same thing happens in Kung's office."

I didn't like the sound of that. "You mean these girls are being eaten?"

Yukina gave her head a quick but firm shake. "Not like

that...What the customers wind up feeding on goes a lot deeper than the girls' flesh."

Ignoring the creepy-crawlies under my skin, I pressed on with, "Prostitution by way of human trafficking?"

Yukina turned her head back around to face me. I could see the sadness dancing in her eyes as she gave her head that same shake. "Believe it or not, it's worse than that. You remember the woman we saw in the tunnel on our way to Kung's office?"

"You mean the geisha?" I asked.

The frown came back on her face. "No geisha would ever wear those clothes. That was a traditional bridal dress." Her voice had a faraway quality to it when she asked, "Have you ever heard of ghost brides, Mr. Vale?"

I drew a blank. "Can't say I have. Doesn't sound good though."

Yukina let something slip into her eyes I hadn't seen all night: vulnerability. "If...you can wait until we meet with this contact of yours, I can explain it to both of you at once."

I nodded, noting we were about a mile from Zian's offsite. "Fine by me. We should be there soon."

———

The offsite was a big, hulking rust-bucket of a building next to the new docks. This seemingly deserted casualty of corporate greed was one of the few places in this city where I'd actually park my car at its destination. Sure, the fancy wheels stick out here too, but Zian regularly sweeps through every private cam in the area to erase any video recording I've ever come by. There are still his private cams on the place but they go straight to his servers at the Indigo, the night-club his family owns in town. Nobody but him—and, I'll admit, his dad—are likely to access those.

Yukina stared up at the building as we got out of the car. "Another warehouse?"

"Shipwright operation," I corrected her, shutting my own door. "It went belly-up during the Great Recession and nobody's been interested in buying it since."

I walked up to the equally rusted front door and waved at the mini-cam over the upper doorframe. "She's part of the job, Zian," I called up. Yukina held up the folder for emphasis. The door buzzed and popped open right after that.

Our steps echoed off the concrete floor inside, each one emphasizing how big and empty the place was now. Smudged windows barely let any outside light in. Metal I-beams that were less corroded than the walls due to the lack of sea air getting to them stood around us like sentinels. The only sign of life was the back office, lit up as though it was getting ready to put in a full workday. Given that dawn couldn't have been more than a couple of hours away, it was close to the truth. I saw a hand wave from the other side of the window when we were halfway to the office.

"Your contact?" Yukina asked.

"Yeah," I confirmed. No sense saying more. Zian had to be experienced to be properly understood.

The office door buzzed as soon as we were close enough and I opened it up for my new acquaintance. The inside of the office was a 1970s relic, all wood panels and hand-me-down furniture. The only things that didn't fit the vibe of the place were the modern laptop on the ancient desk and the guy sitting behind it.

I happen to know Zian had reached his thirtieth birthday not so long ago, yet everything about him seemed to scream "geek teenager". It didn't matter if you were looking at his bright blue eyes, bleach-blonde hair or the weird mix of a grey vest worn on top of a Tron T-shirt, the last thing you'd peg him as was the son of Hermes, the Greek Messenger of the Gods, among other hats.

He opened his mouth to say something but nothing came out as he stared at Yukina. When he closed said mouth to swallow hard, I had a good idea what was going on.

Since I wanted to get something useful done before daybreak, I cleared my throat. "Zian, this is Yukina Tsing, Mad Mao's niece. Ms. Tsing, this is Zianyon, unofficial geek overlord of the Indigo."

That seemed to catch the lady's interest. "You run the Indigo?"

Poor Zian looked more embarrassed than ever. "Um, yeah...I'm sorry, have you been by there before and—"

"*Hai, hai*," Yukina said a bit too fast. "A few times...I love the shooting games."

Zian's eyes brightened at the mention of one of his favorite topics. "You mean like Operation Wolf?"

"Operation Thunderbolt too," Yukina admitted. "My one regret is I can never find a partner to play with on that one."

Sweet as this was, we were on the clock. "I know we're taking a risk meeting here," I interjected.

Zian rubbed the back of his neck and said, "Well, the cat jumped out of the bag when you called me. Now we're all here, fill me in."

We both gave him the basic rundown on Mao's hiring

me, mine and Yukina's meeting at the warehouse, Ms. Wada's offer Kung couldn't refuse, how the woman we'd seen in the tunnel was a ghost bride and the heist we'd been forced to pull off.

Zian leaned back as we finished up. "Funny," he muttered. "I thought they stopped doing ghost brides in the 1940s. Whenever it happens today, they use dolls instead."

"So you *are* familiar with the concept?" Yukina asked, her eyes teetering between impressed and intrigued.

A goofy grin came over Zian's face. "I like to call myself the Prince of Information for a reason."

Actually, I'd been the one to give him that name tag but it seemed a bad time to bring that up. "Anyone mind filling this ignorant *gaijin* in on what ghost brides are all about?"

My young friend smirked at Yukina. "Now you see why he comes to me so often."

"Z..." I said in a tone I used to give my daughter when she was annoying me.

Zian took the hint and raised his hands in surrender. "Alright, alright...The whole ghost bride concept originally came out of China. The idea was that if a young man died before his time, he'd turned that resentment on the living who'd wound up luckier than him. How he'd get back at them comes straight from the Bad Karma Greatest Hits Album: illness, finances going sour, spiritual possession."

"Okay, so how does getting a posthumous marriage certificate him calm down?" I asked, still confused.

"It's more than that," Yukina explained. "Some take our old traditions very seriously and quite literally. When the ceremony is over, the brides are buried alive next to their dead husbands; forced to remain by their side for the rest of eternity."

My mind flashed back to the many pictures I'd seen in Kung's office, as a heavy silence fell on us at her words.

"But you said, they switched to dolls in the 1940s?" I asked.

"Actually, it began in the 1930s," Yukina explained. "The invasion of Manchuria produced a high number of casualties for all those Japanese soldiers and sailors. More young men were dying than there were living potential brides back home."

I picked up the thread right away. "So they came up with a substitute in the form of the dolls."

"With the approbation of our elders." Yukina's jaw tightened as her disgust gave way to anger. "Even so, tradition runs very deep in Japanese culture. There were at least a few families who weren't happy about the change...The kind of families with enough money to make sure the law would never punish them."

I let my own disgust show; I'd seen my fair share of rich assholes getting the get-out-of-jail-free card too.

"So you knew about these families?" Zian wanted to know.

Yukina shook her head. "Heard the rumors. I never believed them until..."

It wasn't just the tightened jaw muscles and the hard swallow which made me ask my next question. I'd seen her body posture too often in the mirror not to recognize it. "Who did you lose?"

She looked over at me, startled. I threw all my pain over my family's deaths into my eyes so she'd understand. She sighed as her jaw muscles relaxed and she nodded. "Ryoka," she said in a near whisper. "She was my best friend. We'd known each other since we were six. She was also the only person who never made fun of my sword obsession. Then, one day, about two years ago..."

She raised her eyes up to the ceiling and snapped her fingers. Opening her hand and using it to make a big wave, she added, "Gone...like she'd never existed. The police found nothing. In time, everybody gave up on her, even her family."

"So you started looking yourself," Zian said.

She let out a deep breath, closed her eyes and nodded. "You have to understand...I was a sheltered girl before. Going to the neighborhoods I did, talking to the people I found there, being told to back off certain questions. They tried to scare me off...it was an education. That's when I decided to do something about all that injustice."

"And your idea to solve all injustice was to become a masked vigilante?" I asked.

"It wasn't like that. I ... I couldn't let them see my face, because of my family, my uncle. I didn't want them getting hurt over me, so I used the scarf. I only had my own agenda; to find out what had happened to Ryoka, but..." She sighed. "...I don't know how, but word got out. It made the local news and people left me messages."

"Messages?" Zian asked.

I understood at once. "All the notes pinned on the corkboard. I wondered about that. How do they give them to you?"

"*Ushi no toki mairi,*" Yukina said, before translating. "Going to worship at the hour of the ox." She sat down on the desk's corner as she explained, "It's an ancient Japanese tale from the Edo period. Rejected women, dressed in white and crowned with an iron ring set with three lit candles, would go out, at two in the morning, the hour of which the ox is the symbol. They'd walk to the nearest Shintô shrine with a straw figure of the lover who abandoned them, and nail it to the nearest sacred tree as they'd pray for the traitor's death."

"Locals came up with a modern version of that sacred message board?" Zian ventured.

"There's a small park in the East of Little Japan. Two benches, a fountain and an old oak tree; people fasten notes to it with iron nails."

"Which the masked vigilante later retrieves at the hour of the ox." I mused.

Yukina nodded. "Something like that."

I was tempted to point out how dangerous it was. If I'd been hired to find the *fukushuu onna* rather than Yukina, I'd have stalked these benches until she showed up—once I figured out that ritual took place, of course.

"Did you ever find her? Your friend?" Zian asked though we both had a good idea of what the answer was.

Yukina shook her head. "For all I know, she's still buried with the dead man she was *married* to." The contempt she put on the word "married" is what someone else would have put on the word "murderer" or "rapist". Taking a deep breath, she concluded, "I couldn't save her. But I am doing my damnedest to save all the others like her."

"Like the woman you saw in the tunnel," Zian said, a sad sympathy playing out over his face.

I felt a similar sadness settle on me like a dark cloud. "Much as I hate to say this, getting the chance to save her is going to require getting the statue for Mao. So why don't we all focus on that?"

"I don't know about that," Zian said, standing up. He raked a nervous hand through his hair. "Seriously, this is taking it too far."

Anger flared up in Yukina's eyes at this statement. "Does my uncle's life mean so little to you?"

"All innocent life means something to me," Zian explained, his British accent flaring up. "But my father has been riding my arse lately. He keeps coming up with new projects and analysis he wants to be done on time and on schedule."

"And you can't squeeze a few minutes to help us do something worthwhile?" I asked, not quite believing my ears.

"Hardly." He turned to me with a pleading expression on his face. "Besides...Bloody hell, Vale. This isn't some data gathering; I'd have no problem with that. But what you want me to do is plan a heist. If Father finds out, I'm dead... or worse."

"Help us plan a heist," I corrected. "There's a difference."

Zian gave me a look somewhere between defeated and angry. "Do you know what Father gave me for my thirtieth birthday? A nice long lecture on how much he wanted me back in the fold and a breakdown of the consequences if I didn't toe his line. That includes frequenting you or winding up on the law's radar again."

I should have been angry at my friend's reply, but I wasn't. I could read between the lines and knew enough of the workings of Alterum Mundum to understand why

Hermes hovered over his son like a vulture who'd smelled blood.

Zian's mother was a mortal, and as a demigod, my hacker friend was soon to be faced with the most difficult choice he'd ever have to make. To stay within the mortal realm and live a normal life or to join the rest of his family in Alterum Mundum for eternity.

My friend's decision was still a coin-toss at this point, but it was easy to guess on which side the Messenger wanted that particular coin to land.

Yukina gently put her hand on top of his and stroked it. "*Kowai mono yotsu: jishin, kaji, kaminari, oyaji.*"

To the unspoken question on Zian's face, she explained, "Something my mother used to say a lot: 'There are four frightening things: earthquake, fire, thunder, and Daddy.'"

"Sounds like she knew my father personally," Zian said with a wry chuckle.

"I realize your father, whoever he is, terrifies you," Yukina went on. "But can you imagine how much being unable to save my uncle terrifies *me*?"

Zian did nothing but breathe for a minute. Then he glanced between me and Yukina and said, "Okay."

"Look, Zian," I said. "I'm sorry if—"

"Forget it, Bell," Zian replied, waving it off as he got back in front of his laptop. "Like the lady implied, I was letting my fear get in the way of my thinking process."

I frowned as a stray thought came out of nowhere. "Yukina, do you have any ideas on what this statue we're supposed to steal represents?"

Yukina frowned as she gave the matter some thought. "Just off the top of my head, I think they were the Four

Mythical Guardians. Each one represents a Cardinal direction as well as other qualities."

"What can you tell me about them?"

"The turtle is Genbu, Guardian of the North. The dragon is Seiryu, Guardian of the East. And the bird could only be Suzaku, Guardian of the South."

I took another look at the statue in the folder. Tapping it, I asked, "What would this tiger be?"

"Byakko, Guardian of the West," she said. "He's also the symbol for righteousness and bravery. I suppose that's appropriate or ironic, given we're planning on stealing him."

I scratched the back of my neck. "Those can't be the only statues of these guardians out there. What makes this set so special?"

Zian looked up from his typing and asked, "Any idea what the statues are made of?"

"Marble," Yukina and I replied at the same time. We both grinned at the synchronicity. I saw Zian smile too as he went back to his staccato attack on his keyboard. The grin vanished the moment his fingers stopped moving.

"Not again," he moaned in despair, rubbing his right hand over his face.

"That bad?" I asked.

"Well, it depends on your opinion of all these statues being in the same room while a certain ritual is going on being able to open up a gate to Alterum Mundum."

"The last time that happened here was bad enough," Yukina said.

I was in the middle of a nod when I wound up doing a doubletake at what she'd said.

"What?" she asked with a shrug. "You think I can be

around my uncle as much as I am without being clued into the supernatural?"

Looking at the equally stunned Zian, she added, "I take it something just as nasty is supposed to come through this gateway?"

"Oh yeah, yeah, definitely," he stammered. "But it gets a little vague on what that could be. The only descriptor I've got is—" He pointed at a word on his screen. "—*this*."

"Scorned Woman," Yukina translated. "That could describe any number of *yokai* and *oni*. None of them are good news."

I let out a frustrated groan. "How many ways to accidentally kill the human race did Alternum Mundum leave over here?"

Yukina held up a finger. "More importantly, what does Ms. Wada gain from inviting such a spirit over here?"

Zian looked between the two of us before suggesting, "Uhm, since we can't answer either one of those questions, how about we take a peek at the museum's schematics for workable ideas?"

8

INITIAL ESTIMATES

For a Thursday afternoon, the museum was surprisingly crowded with people. Then again, it was late enough in the day for people to be off work. The mass suited me fine. It gave us a good layer of non-entities to blend amongst into the background. Now that I'd managed to get some sleep, get a shower and change into a business casual short-sleeved shirt and blue slacks, I looked like any other citizen taking a peek. Yukina opted for her day-job clothes, a conservative-length black skirt and a sheer white blouse. She tied her hair in a ponytail, save for the red strand which she kept tucked behind her ear.

One other contributing factor to the crowd was that the Historical Museum was a recent addition to Cold City. In the aftermath of the downtown bombings, newly-elected Mayor Ian Townsend threw his political clout into establishing events and places which would make this town known for more than tragedy. The fashion show earlier this year was one such push, this museum another.

The building used to be part of the corporate holdings of Townsend's predecessor, a newly demolished site set to build yet another office building. Seizing the property under eminent domain, Townsend had the place turned into the museum we were standing in right now. It was a large but simple two-story structure. Both ends of the building had an open, two-flight staircase with a nearby elevator for those who couldn't or wouldn't walk the steps. The ground floor was a spacious open foyer dominated by paintings from the Stone Age to 20th Century masterpieces. The more compact upper level was encased behind a layer of thick glass that let you look down at the bottom floor. It was mostly a hallway that led to a series of rooms for the more precious pieces the museum could acquire.

The one piece of culture we were interested in was in a display room roughly in the middle of the hallway. Its constrictive twin doorways had open slots around their inside frames, containing the metal doors we saw in the floor plans. The sign over the doorway read *Memories of Edo*, written in golden, flowing script. Yukina glanced at that and shook her head.

"Couldn't they have at least written it in kanji too?" she muttered.

"Who's Edo?" I asked as we stepped into the display room through the left door.

"Not 'who'. Edo was the capital of Japan from 1603 to 1868," she explained once we got into the room. "Tokyo was built on its bones after the Meijis sacked it."

I saw Zian go out the other doorway as we came in, toning down his usual dress sense to look like the college kids he catered to at the Indigo. To the casual observer, he only had eyes and fingers for his iPad. I could hear a live version of the Stones' "Sympathy For The Devil" blasting through his earbuds. But what he was doing was trying to access the museum's Wi-Fi network. If we were lucky, getting control of that would go a long way towards claiming our prize.

Speaking of our prize, it was sitting in the very back of the room. One thing the picture from the folder hadn't shown was that it wasn't alone in its case. An ornate jade mask sat in the center, looking like a demon or Donald Trump on a bad day. The statue sat on the mask's left, while a small crude figurine of a woman holding a baby sat on its right. Three cases apiece lined the left and right walls, each one with a solo example of pottery or vases. Elaborate prints of what I assumed were Edo's heyday took up the upper parts of the walls above those displays.

While all those cases had fluorescent spotlights shining on them, the mask case had natural lighting flowing in from the back windows. Too bad a human wouldn't be able to flow through those windows so easy. A tight set of bars drew a firm line between the inside and the outside. The way this room was facing, the case would get sunlight streaming into it from dawn 'til dusk. That coincided nicely with the end of visiting hours coming up at 6 PM, which was half an hour from now.

I noticed Yukina was bored. "Not your thing?"

She hummed thoughtfully. "If it's not weapons, I don't care."

I could see her point. She likely had seen stuff like this all her life.

I got a look at the gold plate the photo had obscured. It

correctly identified the statue as being Byakko and mentioned how it'd been found in the Okinawa prefecture.

The jade mask stared at all its visitors with the kind of hate I associate with ex-wives. The nameplate below mentioned it was on loan from the Tokyo National Museum and I would be willing to bet my next paycheck that this was hoped to be the first of many such treasures our museum could get from more established collections.

"What's the point of making him that ugly?" I asked Yukina, pointing at the mask.

"To scare people into being good," she answered, her tone telling me she didn't think it worked so well in practice.

"Good like them?" I asked, pointing at the statuette, its nameplate marking it as *Kakure Kirishitan Statuette*.

Yukina's face darkened. "In the Edo period, that was considered anything but good. Those belonged to local Christians."

"There were Christians in Japan that far back?" I asked in fascination.

Yukina nodded. "Part of the Catholic Church's program to undermine the Tokugawa shogunate in charge. No surprise when the shogun's government persecuted the people the church converted."

Even though I had a feeling I knew the answer, I asked, "How bad did it get?"

"It was never good. But it really got bad when the Shimabara Revolt failed. The ones the shogunate didn't kill were forced into exile. The rest went underground." A contemptuous smile crossed her lips. "And after all that, the Catholic Church refused to recognize the dead as martyrs.

Officially, they cited 'materialistic reasons'. Unofficially, I think it had more to do with their race and local politics."

I sighed. No matter what faith you practice, the higher-ups in it always seemed to practice the same powermonger games. And that was before you got into the games they played in Alternum Mundum.

We pretended to look over the displays on the right wall. As spelled out in the schematics, the cameras were in the corners adjacent to the doors. Between the size of the room and the angle of the cameras, there wasn't an inch of this place one or both didn't see. There was a small air vent directly above us in the center, but you'd have to be mouse-sized to be able to squeeze through that.

It wasn't until we exited the room that I spotted something else the blueprints pointed out to us. Inside the door-frame were a couple of black half-orbs at ankle level. Those would have to be the motion detectors. Even if we did manage to somehow get the doors open, they would detect our legs on the way in.

A tour of the next couple of rooms down—which also had artifacts of Japan from earlier periods than Edo—showed considerably less security than the room we needed to break into. It made me scratch my head on what was so valuable in our room that warranted that kind of security.

We spotted Zian at the bottom of the stairs, sitting on a bench with his eyes glued to his iPad. It was no surprise that the bench happened to be sitting across from a room marked "Security Office".

Having done a full sweep of the place, I noted that while there were a few guards here and there, most of the security seemed to be electronic. As Yukina and I made a beeline for the exit, I wondered if it was good news.

———

"I'm afraid the news is not good," Zian said.

We just made it back to his offsite. We hung around an hour after the museum closed by going to a restaurant across the street. Zian covered our meal with what looked like a company credit card and insisted we get a window seat. We ate slowly enough to see the time it took for all the daytime staff to leave and the nighttime security to come on shift. Now we were back in Zian's retro office going over what we'd found.

"Define 'not good'," I requested, dreading what he might say.

"Whoever put their in-house network together knew what they were doing. The security system is on a closed network that can't be accessed remotely."

"But not un-hackable, *hai*?" Yukina asked.

That made Zian grin for a second. "No such beast exists." The grin faded as he added, "The problem is that to be able to do so requires physical access."

"Like, say, the security station you were sitting next to when we made our exit?" I asked.

"In one, Bell," Zian confirmed, pointing at me. "I'm afraid that's not the end of the bad news either."

I leaned back in my seat and groaned at the ugly, off-white ceiling. "What?"

"Well, so far as I can tell, I can take care of the cameras

and motion detectors once I have access. However, that is not true of the pressure sensors on the floor."

"That wasn't in the plans," Yukina noted with surprise.

"Might have been a last minute addition to beef up the security in that room," Zian speculated. "The only reason I know about them is because of an in-house email I grabbed that mentioned them."

"And you can't shut them down?" I asked, tilting my head to look at Zian again.

"Not according to the email's author," Zian said with a frown of his own. "In fact, he complained a lot on how the sensors were on their own system and how the slightest pin drop would set off the alarm."

"But why that room?" I growled in frustration. "I get it: valuable artifacts some enterprising thief might want to steal. But that room had more protection than any of the others."

"The mask," Yukina speculated, stroking her chin. "Remember, it's on loan. The Tokyo National Museum likely wanted extra security."

"Considering the current value on it is $40 million, that'd be my guess too," Zian confirmed.

I rubbed my face. "We've got to find out more about those floor sensors."

Yukina looked at Zian with a question. "Taking care of the rest would still be easier?"

"Sure, assuming we could finagle our way into the security area," Zian said. "Best way I could think of would be a bit of *sweet talkin'*."

I froze at Zian's last two words, or rather at the way he'd said them, with a faked, forced Texan accent. It all but spelled out what he had in mind. "No...Don't even think about it."

"Why not?" he replied, unfazed by my refusal. "It's not like any of us could bedazzle our way into that room."

"No—just, no!" I persisted, keeping my finger up. "Bringing her on is a risk I won't take."

Zian's face got stony. "If you have a better plan, I'm all ears. We've burned through twelve hours we're never getting back. So wasting any more time is a bigger risk."

I wasn't sold. "Art theft, Zian! We've done some borderline things with her. But this is way past all that."

"Oh, come on, Bell," Zian said with his trademark goofy grin. "You think Candice would pass up a chance like this? First on the scene the next day, exclusive report."

"Candice?" Yukina asked, not getting it.

"Candice Kennedy," I explained. "A reporter friend, *and* the last person who needs to be called in for something like this."

"Again, if you've got a better idea, now's the time to bring it up."

I glowered at Zian. He knew I didn't have one, and time was running out. I couldn't help but think of Mao, and pictured him in his little shop, going about his day without knowing the danger he was in. He'd trusted me to help him, and I'd all but painted a bullseye on his back in return. But this? Oh, but this was going to come bite me on the ass later.

I pulled out my phone and dialed up Kennedy's number, putting it on speaker.

The journalist answered on the second ring. "Hey, hoss, long time, no hear," the honey-sweet voice said on the other end. "So I'm guessing something's up?"

"Yeah, we need a favor," I said, giving Zian a glower. He merely shrugged in response.

"This favor happens to be attached to a story I might find more than a little juicy?" she wanted to know, sounding practically turned on by the prospect.

I gave the phone a nervous look. "It's looking like it, yeah. But I should warn you...This one's a bit more over the line than usual."

The sweet Texas accent rang out in her high-pitched laughter. "Well, hell, Bell, I'd be disappointed in you and Zian if it wasn't. That *is* who you meant by the 'we', right?"

"There's someone else on this too," I mentioned, looking over at Yukina. She looked at the phone and then me with a smirk.

"Client?" Kennedy asked.

"Sort of, kind of, but not really," I said, not sure how I'd define the relationship at this point. "It's a long story."

"Usually is with you, hoss. So...now we've beaten the ground 'round the bush hard enough, what's that favor of yours?"

Zian had that one covered. "How's your acting skills, dear?"

9

MOTHER OF THE YEAR

The next morning, I found myself sitting alone behind Zian's desk, looking at his laptop monitor. The screen had a couple of windows open showing live footage of the museum security feed. I focused on the bottom two, which came from moving body cams. From the images I could see, the two people who wore them were in sight of the museum's entrance.

I drummed my fingers on the desk as I stared at the screen, feeling useless. Hitting the talk switch on the mic stand to the laptop's right, I said into it, "Somebody want to explain to me once again why I'm on monitor duty? It wouldn't be the first time I've cased a place without being noticed."

Zian's voice came up from the laptop speakers, his British accent distorted by the electronics. "Oh, don't be so cross about it, Bell. Someone needs to keep an eye on the house while we're gone." On the monitor, I saw he gave the camera he was wearing a thumbs-up. "Just don't touch anything and you'll do great."

I raised an eyebrow at the screen.

A little girl's voice broke the background noise an instant later, "When can we play, Aunti—I mean, Mommy?"

"Soon, honey, real soon," Kennedy's voice said back to her in a soothing tone that'd put an irate cobra to sleep. "But we've got to get inside first, okay?"

"Okay," the little girl's voice replied. I couldn't see her face, but the bright and chipper smile on it was plain to hear.

My phone buzzed in my pocket. I pulled it out to see it was a text from Yukina. The message was straight to the point: *Yes*.

Flipping on the mic again, I said, "Heard back from our mutual friend...We can take care of that other problem easy."

"Well, that's nice to hear," Zian replied, entering the museum ahead of Kennedy and the kid. "It's one less part of the plan to worry about."

"But you knew that already, didn't you?" I asked, wanting to confirm a suspicion. "This was designed to keep her busy while we did the dirty work."

"Oh, don't tell me you boys pulled some of that macho 'protect the women' crap," Kennedy said through her own earpiece.

"Who are you talking to, Mommy?" the little girl asked as they stepped through the entrance.

"Just a friend who needs to know how to treat a lady, Andy," Kennedy replied.

"Oh, c'mon, you lot!" Zian protested, his cam taking in the Security Office entrance before moving on. "The Avenging Woman has enough people looking for her on both sides of the law, the last thing she needs is to be seen on the museum's cameras footage hours before a major break-in. The same can be said about you, Bell."

Kenney's body cam showed her wandering around the first floor, while it seems Zian was walking up the right stairs to get to the second floor.

"I wonder if she'll agree to an interview when this is over," Kennedy mused as she stopped in front of some abstract paintings. "I could be the Lois Lane to her Superman."

I snorted, glad my finger was off the switch. I know quite a few hells that would have to freeze over first before Yukina agreed to go anywhere near a journalist.

"As much as I enjoy the picture this metaphor inspired, I wouldn't try that one out," Zian said, as he reached the top.

I hummed into the mic. "I second both of these thoughts."

"Macho pigs," Kennedy huffed, under her breath, "Narrow-minded macho pigs."

"Are your friends being mean, Mommy?" Andy asked.

Kennedy chuckled. "Ahh, a little mean, honey, which is why I'm tellin' them to drop it."

Kennedy's cam went lower while she knelt down, finally capturing an image of the child she'd borrowed for the day. She was a sweet-faced little girl of about six, curly dark blonde hair with a bit of baby fat on her face. The cam got way close to her chest for a second, followed by the distinctive smack of a kiss on the forehead.

"Now...you remember what I said about being a good girl?" Kennedy asked her.

Andy nodded with a grin on her face.

"Okay, I'm going to leave you right here," she said, standing back up. "I'll be back in a few minutes. Just like we practiced, okay?"

"Okay, Mommy," Andy said. Her blue eyes were bright with eagerness. The cam turned away from the little girl and walked up the left staircase.

"You're certain involving your godchild is the best idea?" Zian asked, his cam capturing her walking the steps.

"Oh, we're like two peas in a pod," she said in a low voice. "Her mom Jenny's always glad when I can get a day to take Andy off her hands. It gives her a break from parenting so she can recharge her batteries."

"Well, if you are so alike, I'm guessing she didn't do this for free?" I asked into the mic.

Kennedy chuckled again. "Let's just say Jenny's gonna be *really* upset on how many chocolate chip cookies I send her daughter home with today."

The phone buzzed again...Yukina. The message this time was wordier: *Anything else?*

I texted Yukina back with, *Come to the offsite.*

By this point, Kennedy was passing Zian. My hacker buddy had changed his look to that of a young professional accountant or something. His bleached blond hair was neatly combed backwards and held in place with hair-gel. He was wearing a pearl grey three-piece suit, clear glasses and a black tie.

I knew he'd be slipping Kennedy a small device half the size of her palm as she walked past.

"Well, I'm ready to go," Zian said, confirming his little package was delivered.

"Time to go find your little girl," I said to Kennedy.

"Way ahead of you," my reporter friend assured me, her steps taking her down the opposite staircase.

As planned, Andy had long since left the spot Kennedy had left her at. "Andy?" Kennedy asked, putting the right twinge of panic in her voice. "Andy, where are you, darling?"

The video stream grew frantic as Kennedy cased the ground floor left and right. She made quick strides around the area, repeating Andy's name in an increasingly anguished tone. While Kennedy caught everyone's attention, Zian's body cam showed him fiddling with the iPod he'd pulled from his outer coat pocket. A program was booting up on it, showing a progress bar of 57% and climbing.

"Almost good," Zian said. Meanwhile, Kennedy was doing her best impersonation of a distraught mother, running from one end of the area to the other. Having been around more than a few hysterical mothers myself, I had to say she was convincing. A few seconds later, the progress bar on Zian's iPod came up to 100%. "Ready when you are," he breathed. That was all Kennedy needed to hear to make a run for the Security Office.

Once she got there, she pounded on the door. "Please, anyone, please, I need help!" Her voice was down-right sobby at this point, and I bet she turned on the waterworks. It took three more sets of hysterical knocks for the door to open.

A middle-aged, paunchy security guard in a white uniform was waiting on the other side. "What's the matter, ma'am?" he asked in a bass voice.

"Please, sir, oh please, it's my little girl," Kennedy said, playing up the tears and desperation that would have done credit to Meryl Streep. "I can't find her anywhere and I've looked and looked and looked!"

While she was saying this, the guard scratched at his beard nervously. "Tell you what..." he said, ushering her inside, more to put an end to the scene that had caught everyone's attention than anything else, "I'm not supposed to do this but if you want, we can see if we can spot her on the monitors."

Kennedy gasped a bit at the offer. "Oh, thank you. Thank you!"

The inside of the security station came up on screen. Half a dozen monitors were affixed to the wall, each with its own stream of visitors ambling about the museum. A large desk sat in front of it.

I had to admit the camera coverage of the place was impressive. If we didn't have Zian's technical know-how to get past them, I had no problem believing we'd get caught about ten seconds after breaking in.

"Alright, ma'am," the guard said off-camera. "Calm down, take your time and look. I know there's a lot of people flowing through the building, but—"

"I'll know it's her the second I see her," Kennedy said, keeping the trembling edge in her voice going. The convincing performance she was putting on made me wonder if she'd studied drama before switching up to journalism. After all, she *was* a model once, which is usually most actresses' first step towards their career.

"Simply place the package anywhere," Zian said to Kennedy through his earpiece. "If it's close, I'll see it."

Kennedy's body cam did a heavy tilt towards the security panel.

"Ma'am, are you alright?" the guard asked, his shadow coming into frame from the right.

I saw the subtle movement on her left hand that told me she was clipping Zian's device under the counter. To the guard, she said, "Yes, I'm...well, 'okay' isn't the right word but... Sorry, a dizzy spell."

"Of course," the guard said with understanding. He manhandled Kennedy back to the monitors. "Just look at those screens, okay?"

With all the people in the museum, I had to admit I had a hard time spotting Andy myself. Of course, there was the added complication I was looking at the cams through yet another screen. Kennedy had to have an easier time of it.

My reporter accomplice screeched and pointed a finger at the upper right screen. "There! That's her! That's my Andy."

"Okay, that's the rightmost room on the second floor," the guard said. "If she's not there by the time you get in, come back here and we'll find her again, okay?"

"Okay, thank you so much!" Kennedy said as she tore her way to the door.

"How's the hookup coming, Zian?" I asked through the mic.

"It's always easier to show than to tell," Zian replied right before a new window automatically opened up on the laptop. It began as a blank black space before a live feed popped up in squares all over it.

"How's reception?" my friend asked, his body cam showing him standing up.

"Coming in crystal-clear," I said with a grin. "Time to head home."

"What and miss the final act?" Zian asked back. I could hear a grin of his own in his voice.

I glanced over at Kennedy's bodycam and saw Andy walking back onto the second floor balcony from the room on the furthest right. Kennedy made a joyful noise as she ran over to her borrowed little girl, sweeping her up in a hug. Naturally, I didn't see anything but an extreme close up of Andy's t-shirt when that happened.

"Oh, Andy. I was so worried about you, honey," my partner said loud enough to be heard.

"Was I a good girl?" I heard the little one whisper into the hug.

"A real good girl, Andy," Kennedy replied in the same tone. "You earned them cookies fair and square."

Once the hug was over, Andy made her lip quiver and stared at the floor. "I'm sorry, Mommy. I know I should have stayed downstairs but—"

"Oh, never mind all that, sweetie," Kennedy said to her, grabbing her hand. "Let's get home now, okay? I think we've had more than enough excitement for one day."

Andy looked up at Kennedy slow and deliberate. "You're not mad at me?"

"Oh, a little bit, but we'll talk about it when we get home, alright?"

The little girl's eyes went back to the floor. "Yes, Mommy."

As everybody headed for the exit, I was left to wonder if Andy would pursue the acting career as Kennedy should have.

———

"For what that apartment building charges renters, you'd think security would be better," Yukina remarked later that night at the offsite, standing in front of the desk.

"Sweetie, I can tell you," Kennedy said, sitting down with her eyes glued to a tablet which had the area around the museum on display, "I ain't never met no landlord who didn't try cutting corners to make a few extra bucks."

I looked up from the museum plans in my own seat to tell Yukina, "Add in the fact this particular apartment building is next to a museum instead of, say, a meth house, and the owners probably don't see the need for extra security."

Yukina paced around the tiny space of the office. "That's the kind of complacency criminals count on."

Zian's eyes stayed fixed on his laptop while he did his usual speed typing routine as he said, "Statistically, it's one of the lowest crime areas in Cold City...The perfect magnet for upscale professionals like you, remember?"

Yukina's pacing increased as she shook her head. "No interior cams, a back door with a lock from the 1950s, no doorman after 6 PM and a roof adjacent to every building around it...To me, it's a giant bullseye."

"Well, that's why we wanted you to scout that," I replied with a shrug. "Now we know it's a safe way to get into the museum."

Yukina stopped pacing and raised an eyebrow at me. "Planning on leaping tall buildings in a single bound?"

"Harpoon and rope," Zian replied. "It's got the right elevation and angle for us to zipline down. Thanks to our new Wi-Fi enabled hookup, I'll be able to pop the roof door open for you."

"There's still those floor sensors to deal with," I reminded my hacker buddy.

"And if we had time, I could work something out. As it stands, you'll have to improvise."

"One other thing y'all might not have thought about," Kennedy said, looking up from the tablet. "If we go and grab the one piece we're after, that's gonna raise a lot of questions we don't need asked."

Yukina gave Kennedy a sharp look. "I am not a thief."

Kennedy held up a hand. "Not saying you are, Yuki, but you want to—"

The katana on Yukina's back was pointing at Kennedy's face in an eye blink. "The name is Yukina. I won't remind you again."

True to her roll-with-it nature, my favorite lady reporter took the blade in stride. "Fair enough. Seeing as I don't like folks calling me 'Candy', I should have known better. I do apologize."

Yukina sheathed the sword but looked confused. "You didn't seem intimidated."

Kennedy chuckled. "No offense, honey, but I've been up against way scarier things since I meet these two." She pointed at me and Zian for emphasis.

"Getting back to what Kennedy was saying," I said, glad the crisis was averted. "I'm guessing you caught the gist of what she was proposing?"

"And I still don't like it," the swordswoman affirmed with a glare.

"The only thing worse than a crime with too few clues is one with too many," Kennedy explained. "So if we grab a few extra pieces along with the one we're after, the cops suddenly got a lot more interesting things to go look for."

"And what are *we* supposed to do with the extras?" Yukina asked, looking between me and Kennedy.

"Here's what I'd do," Zian chimed in. "I'd give them to a fence I didn't like, figure out where he'd be holding the goods, call in an anonymous tip and let him take the fall."

Yukina gave the plan some thought. "One problem," she said. "He could still give us up."

"Not if it could be traced to some thieves who just pulled a score and deserved to go down too," I added. "Think you could set that up, buddy?"

Zian shrugged. "Give me some names to work with, shouldn't be a problem."

Yukina looked up at the white plaster ceiling, tapping her foot in thought. When she turned back at Zian, she said, "I might have those names."

"Well, while you kids are working that out," Kennedy said, standing up from her seat. "Me and Bell here need to talk about some important stuff. We'll be outside."

"We will?" I asked while Kennedy made for the office door. She gave me an annoyed look followed by a quick jerk of her head towards the abandoned factory floor. Taking the hint, I got up, left the plans on the chair and walked her way. I couldn't miss Zian's cheeky smile as he buzzed open the door for us to exit.

Once we got outside, Kennedy didn't stop moving until we were in the middle of the concrete sea. When she turned around, I asked, "Alright, what's so important you wanted to be out of earshot?"

Kennedy shrugged. "Nothing ...I figured they'd want to have some private time to themselves is all."

I did my best to play dumb. "You mean those two are—"

"Oh, goddamn it, Bell. If you don't see it by now, you're a lousier detective than even I think sometimes."

"Thanks," I said with heavy sarcasm.

Kennedy's face went from mocking to serious. "Look, our boy's way too sheltered for a man his age. Do him some good to hook up with a no-bullshit woman like Yukina, who can make him see past his monitors."

I had to admit it made sense, given how sheltered Yukina was herself. Still, I asked Kennedy, "And what makes you think our samurai warrior woman is receptive to this little bit of matchmaking?"

"Well, look at how she flew off the handle at me back in there. You only get that kind of anger if you feel alone in this world. It ain't a good place to be and unlike some other fool men I've dated, Zian's sharp enough to know better than to try and change her."

I looked at them through the office window. Yukina was leaning awfully close over Zian's shoulder while he stayed glued to the monitor. They didn't look like they were on the verge of a kiss. But stay in my line of work long enough and you can spot intimacy from orbit.

"Heard about you and Ramirez, hoss," Kennedy added, her voice a little sadder. "And I'm sorry as hell you two ain't together no more."

I stared at her in surprise. "Where'd you hear that from?"

The reporter shrugged. "Straight from the source...Me and Ramirez have been friendly since that fool jinn tried hijacking the both of us for his harem."

"Well, technically, he was trying to marry both of you," I corrected her, shuddering at the memory of how close he came to success.

"Like there's a damn difference?" Kennedy snapped. "Anyhow, it won't surprise you to hear she's still got a crap-load of questions about all that."

"What if she does?" I asked with a shrug. "The beat we walk falls outside CCPD's jurisdiction, especially when it comes to a cleared case like that one."

Kennedy licked her lips while glancing at the floor. Her voice took a more serious tone, as she said: "She's having nightmares."

I felt a little chill. "What kind of nightmares?"

"The kind that sound a lot like memories of everything the smoky bastard put us through," Kennedy replied. "She don't want to talk to a shrink, can't talk to her boss, so she wound up talking to me."

"Given the way you two met..." I said, flashing back to Ramirez running into us at Sundowner's Café by accident.

"Yeah, I brought that one up myself. But she worked out you and me have never been a thing. Combine that with me being the only other person she knew who'd understand and we've been talking ever since." Hesitation filtered on Kennedy's face as she paused. I waited as she made up her mind on whether she should keep talking to me or not. "She's starting to lose it, Bellamy. She doesn't want to believe the memories are real, but what other option is there. It's either they're real or she's going crazy."

I felt a stab of guilt in my gut over this new information. "You know why I can't tell her."

My boss, Lady McDeath, gave me an earful when she

found out I'd spilled the beans to Kennedy about Alterum Mundum—and by earful, I mean grabbed me by the throat and almost killed me. I dreaded to think what she'd do to me if I brought someone else in on it. Not to mention the danger it would put Ramirez in.

"She's in an impossible situation and I hate seeing her like that. So either you tell her or I'll help her figure it out on her own. Either way, she's gonna know soon enough."

I felt my jaw tighten up. "I already lost one woman I loved. I'm likely to lose another one if she ever finds out the truth."

Kennedy gave me a thoughtful look before answering. "My mama's mama, God rest her soul, drilled this into my head when I was a kid: 'Ignorance ain't bliss, hiding ain't protecting and secrets ain't forever'. You might want to think on that."

We stayed quiet while I looked back over at Zian and Yukina. She was sitting beside him now and I could tell they were both chatting animatedly with each other. Why couldn't I find a relationship like that since my family died?

Kennedy got my attention again by clearing her throat. Pointing at the tablet, she said, "Think I got just the right spot for a getaway car."

10

WRONG TURN

I took careful aim with the harpoon gun. Last time I used one of these, I was still in the Navy. Through the Starlight scope on top of it, I had the rooftop doorway dialed in nice and tight. I could make out the mini-cam sitting over it.

"Okay, cameras are on the loop," Zian said into my earpiece. "Fire when ready, Gridley."

While marveling that he knew that century-old saw, I gently pulled the trigger. A burst of compressed air spat out the harpoon, hitting the center of the scope's bullseye effortlessly. I pulled my face away from the scope and handed the gun to Yukina. Like me, she was dressed in all black, right down to subbing out her trademark red face scarf for a black one. Unlike her, I opted for an old-school ski mask that covered everything on my head but the eyes.

My partner pulled the gun back, making the rope between it and the harpoon as tight as she could. She asked, "Where is the switch again?"

"Left side, couple of inches from the muzzle," Zian explained.

After getting a grip on the rope, Yukina hit the switch and pulled the extended line free of the gun. She handed the gun back to me so I could reload it with the other harpoon/rope combo laying on the ground.

"How's our exit looking?" I asked into the earpiece.

"We good, hoss," Kennedy's voice replied. "Just get out to where I am and we'll all be gone before anyone knows it."

I slung the harpoon gun over my shoulder. While I rechecked the pitch-black backpack lying next to where the harpoon reload was, I noticed Yukina anchoring the rope into the lip of the apartment building roof. She used some small nails she hammered in with a rubber mallet. She rechecked the tautness after she was done. Satisfied, she handed me the hammer so I could repack it in the backpack.

"You're sure this thing will hold our weight?" I asked, pulling a black leather belt out from the pack.

"Spider silk with a Teflon coating," Yukina replied, grabbing a leather belt from the pack herself. "It could hold three times our combined weight."

Not that I doubted her, but it struck me we were in for a hard three-story drop if she got that—or the nailing down of the rope—wrong.

Still, the zipline move was a lot less eventful than I feared. Two seconds of sliding down while hanging on for dear life and we were both on the museum's roof with no extra worries. I grabbed a hold of the harpoon and got it loose from the doorframe in a few hard yanks. After that, I threw it back towards the building, watching the rope arc towards an apartment window. I winced when I heard the slight crack of window glass, but no lights came on in the building so I got back to business.

"Pop the lock?" I asked.

"Door is no-go," Zian came back, sounding urgent. "Guard incoming on your position in about fifteen seconds. Switch to Route B."

I did my best to suppress an exasperated sigh. And here I hoped we were done with relying on ropes to get into this place.

Yukina seemed a lot less upset at this development while she tugged at my arm. She guided us towards the rooftop skylight behind the door. She pulled a coil of rope which ended with a plastic anchor from the pack. I focused on the latch at the base of the skylight. This one didn't have a lock to break.

I'd just opened our new entrance when we both heard the door swing open behind us.

"He's heading away from your position," Zian said. "Going towards the apartment building...He's on a smoke break. Be quiet and he shouldn't notice you."

Nonplussed, Yukina attached the anchor to the side of the skylight and let the rope fall. When I heard the rope hit something below, I yanked out the harpoon gun to check out things through the scope. No sign of the smoking guard coming our way, so I pointed it down below. The end of the line landed on the floor of the second-story balcony, no sign of any guards around.

"Balcony below is clear," Zian told us, confirming my recon. "Go."

As I slung the gun back over my shoulder, my partner went head-first down the rope, shimmying her way to the bottom upside-down. A falling leaf makes more noise than she did when she flipped herself back into a standing position below. Being a lot less of an athlete than her, I went over the side feet-first, doing everything I could to ignore all the little noises I was making as I slid down. I felt the rope try to burn its way through my gloves, Teflon coating or not. Once I touched the bottom, Yukina grabbed the rope and whipped it hard enough to make a wave go through it. It took two more of those to get the anchor loose from the window. I caught it before it could hit the floor as hard as I did.

We both looked around to get ourselves oriented. We were standing in front of the room closest to the right staircase. It was sealed up tight for the night, thanks to the same kind of security doors our target room had. On the other side of the balcony, I heard footsteps going down the left staircase and spotted a few flashlight beams on the ground floor.

"Everybody's somewhere else," Zian informed us. "We're good for the next two minutes and change."

Both Yukina and I did another quick scan to verify that last statement.

"Oh, get on now," Zian growled into the mic. "All you're doing is wasting valuable seconds."

I looked at Yukina and shrugged. He did have a point. My partner nodded and padded her way to the Edo exhibit room. Her soft slipper shoes made as much noise as an evening breeze. By contrast, my rubber boots made quiet squeaks and thuds with each step.

As expected, the doors were sealed tight against all intruders. "In position," Yukina whispered.

"Yeah, I see you," Zian verified from his end of the comm. "Give me a second to open the door just right."

That confused me. "What do you mean 'just right'?" I asked in a voice that tried to be as quiet as my partner's.

"I open it up all the way, someone might notice from the bottom," Zian explained with more patience than I would have had in his position. "So I need to crack it enough for the both of you to slip in."

"And how many of those valuable seconds you mentioned will *that* take?" Yukina said with clear disgust.

"I don't know," Zian admitted. "I've been working on it since you were up on the roof. Think I'm close now."

Oh, this got better and better. "You think?"

"Steady on...Come my way a little, luv...and bingo!"

The left door lurched a little, leaving a perfect crack for us to squeeze through. Unfortunately, it also made a scraping sound which echoed off the glass and walls around us.

"What the hell?" a guard muttered from the bottom of the left staircase.

"In!" I grunted at Yukina but as usual, she was ahead of me.

She slipped her way into the room, leaving me to play catch-up. I handed her the gun before making my own entry. It turned out to be a tighter fit than I anticipated, making me work to get in. I finally came out the other side but I was off-balance enough to make me tip over. I found myself staring at the rapidly approaching floor before something stopped my fall...Yukina. I marveled at the strength in her tiny arms as she helped me regain my footing. The door promptly shut behind us, making a lot less noise than when it opened.

I could make out some footsteps that came to a halt in

front of the door. "Don't think the loop is going to help us here if the security cam guy is watching," I pointed out.

"Already got some footage from earlier captured," Zian assured me. "Just sit still for a minute."

Yukina pressed her ear to the door to listen more closely. I heard something that resembled a muffled human voice. Putting my own ear to the wall, I was able to make out, "Nah, nothing, Control. Guess I was hearing things. Goddamn, I really need to get to the ear doc..."

When the steps went off to the right, I sighed with relief. Under her scarf, I thought I could see Yukina break out in a smile. We both looked into the room to take stock. A gibbous moon was shining its light through the back window behind our target display case. It gave the place an eerie feel, like we were raiding a Shintô temple instead of a modern museum.

"Where do the floor sensors start?" Yukina asked into her earpiece.

"On the first tiles past the doorway," Zian explained. "The second you put pressure on any of those, they'll know you're here."

I tapped the right wall next to me. It was painted to look like marble, but the texture on it was drywall. "Think we've got an anchor point for the ropes here. Where's a good place to shoot the harpoon to?"

"Any place on the back wall should do the trick," Zian said. "Nobody thought to put any sensors on those."

This time, I could spot a frown under Yukina's mask. "I know you're not looking forward to this part," I told her gently. "Believe me, if there was another way—"

She handed me the backpack and raised the harpoon

gun in one motion. "I believe you," she replied. "I don't like it."

A second later, the harpoon went flying to the left side of the window, burying itself deeper than it had the roof. Once again, she detached the rope, pulled it taut and made double sure it was firmly anchored. While she did, she handed me the gun. I pulled out the next harpoon/rope combo from the pack. Once it was ready to fire again, I shot my own harpoon towards the right side of the window. I could hear Yukina softly tapping in the nails while I pulled my own rope tight.

She gave me a sharp "Psst!" to prompt me to move aside so she could nail in this rope too.

"Going by the camera feed and the blueprints," Zian said. "Both those ropes are firmly lodged in the load-bearing beams of that wall. Should be able to support your weight as the roofs outside did."

Yukina sighed while she drove in the last nail. "Let's get this over with."

She took the right rope and climbed across it upside-down with the grace of a chimpanzee. I did the same on the left rope with considerably less grace and the backpack slung across my back weighing me down. I hadn't done anything like this since Basic. The queasy feeling in my stomach and the blood rushing from my head told me why I never bothered trying for the SEALs.

Still, I kept enough presence of mind to gently set the backpack on top of the case when I got close. Just the same, I didn't dare set myself down even though Yukina had done so.

"What are you waiting for, Bell?" Zian asked through the comm. "That glass is strong enough to hold your weight."

I took a deep breath as I cautiously tried for a dismount. I lowered my legs, twisting my hips around to where they touched the top of the case. I shifted my arms around to where I could complete the dismount. Yukina crept over to me but I shook my head at her. "I got it," I assured her before I let go of the rope. My knees hit the case, followed by my hands. I knelt over the tiger inside and tried to catch my breath. I wiped all the flop sweat I accumulated on the way over onto my pants.

Out of a hidden pocket in her right pant leg, Yukina pulled out a pair of scalpels. I could see the slight sheen of diamond on the blade of the one she handed me. With my free hand, I gave her four packets of bubble wrap, all of them big enough for the vases.

After she tucked the bubble wrap under her arm, she turned around and made a quiet running jump for the nearest vase case. She landed on it with the poise of a professional gymnast, but she didn't stop there. She kept going, leapfrogging her way from case to case until she reached the one nearest the door. Once she got there, she dropped to her knees to cut open the glass.

"Any alarms?" I asked Zian.

"Yeah, but their Wi-Fi signals are blocked from the security mainframe," he assured me. "You may slice with impunity."

By the time he said that, Yukina had extracted the vase and slid it into one of the bubble wrap packages. She gave me a quick hiss before pointing at the other side of the case I was sitting on. I crawled over and she held the vase aloft. Once both my hands were ready to catch it, she threw it over like it was a softball. The delicate antique hit my hands like a fly ball and I wasted no time putting it in the backpack.

We repeated this process as she worked her way back over to the other three vases. Then I backed up enough for her to get back to my case. While she made her jump, I checked the vases to make sure they were safe from breakage. She landed with a dull thump and instructed, "Next set."

I pulled out four more bubble wrap packages, which she promptly took before turning a little cartwheel over me to get to the case's right side. Why hadn't this woman ever tried out for the Olympics? Of course, that thought prompted a lot of other more sexual possibilities I shoved into a corner. We were on the clock right now.

I cut into the glass above the Kakure Kirishitan statue. Given the history Yukina told me, I wondered how much the Japanese authorities would be upset by it being broken. But that wasn't my call or my mission, so I slipped it into a bubble wrap packet like Yukina was doing with the vases. I had a special-sized packaging for the mask I cut free next, both big enough and flat enough to accommodate it. Once I got close to Yukina's row of vase cases, she had her latest covered ceramic ready to throw. We played another four games of catch-the-invaluable-antique before she got back to me.

Both of us looked down anxiously at the statue that was our true target. "You know," Yukina said. "I'm more nervous about taking this one than I was the rest."

"Me too," I assured her. "And believe me when I say it's the smart attitude to have."

By silent, mutual consent, we placed our scalpel edges

on opposite sides of the statue. We carefully carved out a circle over it together. She caught the glass before it could hit the tiger itself, laying it aside before grabbing her side of it. When I grabbed the other, we gently lifted it up and she wound up holding onto it when it was lifted out of the case. While Yukina put it in our last bubble wrap packet, I opened a big, roomy side pocket on the outside of the backpack's open flap. The statue slid in there like a glove, even if it made pulling the zipper over it more of a struggle than I had anticipated.

Once the backpack's main compartment was zipped up, Yukina put it over her small shoulders. She sighed again. "I will never outlive this shame," she muttered. Before I could say anything comforting, she was back on the rope and shimmying her way across. I waited until she was in the doorway before I followed suit.

Getting off the rope on the doorway was a lot less complicated than it was at the case end. I made my feet let go of the rope, swung them back towards the doorway and made my hands let go before my feet hit the floor a little hard. I winced at the noise but nothing gave me any sign something bad was about to happen.

Putting a hand to my earpiece, I said to Zian, "Please tell me you've got a less noisy way to exit this room."

"You saw the same blueprints I did," Zian argued. "So you'll be going out the same way you went in. I'll time it a little better to where they can't hear you, though."

"How soon?" Yukina asked him.

"Thirty seconds starting now," Zian replied.

In my head, I began my own version of the countdown,

hoping this would go a lot smoother than the last round. I had a second to go on my count when the door lurched again. I went first this time. I had a few extra inches to squeeze through that let me keep the harpoon gun slung over my shoulder. Yukina handed me the backpack before squeezing out of the door as casually as if it were wide open. When the door snapped closed again, I took stock of the situation. There were a couple of flashlight beams below but none pointed our way. Up here, it was just us, the dead motion detectors and the blind cameras.

"Alright, the route to the evac point is clear," Zian told us. "You've got three minutes to get there."

"Keys in the ignition," Kennedy chimed in. "Soon as the door opens, I'll turn the engine over."

Staying below the banister level, both of us slinked down the right staircase. I crawled down the steps while Yukina continued to prove her flexibility by crab-walking the whole way down. Just a few minutes more and this lousy errand would be in our rearview mirror.

Everything was going good until we got near the last exhibit room before the exit. No, a guard didn't spot us. No, we didn't trip some alarm Zian had missed. No, we hadn't made any noise that got security's attention. What happened was I saw something I shouldn't have.

The room was stocked with exhibits of ancient Greece, as I could tell by the art style on the vases and plates on display. But what had caught my attention wasn't either of those. It was a crude black statuette of a woman, her features hard to make out in the gloom. But there was no way I couldn't make out the material it was made from...Painite, the same as the small bident tool I had received, courtesy of my boss Lady McDeath. It was one of the rarest gemstones on Earth, costing up to $60,000 per carat.

The brand Lady McDeath planted on my shoulder burned at the sight, telling me it was important. Since we'd stolen this many artifacts and were close to the entrance anyway, what was one more on our way out the door? And with that impulsive decision, the night went to hell.

11

BREAKING AND EXITING

When I drifted over to the Greek exhibits room, Zian was the first to call me on it. "Bell, what are you doing?"

"Saw something," I told him, my eyes fixed on the statue. "It may be important."

No sealed doors or motion detectors in this room. Near as I could tell, there was only one camera in it too, back right corner and facing the door.

"Not to tell you your business, hoss," Kennedy chimed in. "But now's a lousy time to change up the plan."

"Won't take a second," I told her, digging out the diamond-edged scalpel from my pants pocket. Surely the glass around it worked on the same alarm system as the cases we'd cut through upstairs.

I was nearly in front of the statue when a hand grabbed me by the shoulder and its owner hissed some stern Japanese words at me.

The alarmed and disgusted tone Yukina used required

no translation. But I shrugged off her shoulder and stepped onto the tile in front of the statue...Which shall hereafter be referred to as Mistake Number One.

My foot had barely put pressure on the tile when the alarm went off.

"Shit," I snapped, taking my foot off the spot way after it mattered. Guess the floor sensors hadn't been confined to the Edo room.

"We need to go!" Yukina whispered, grabbing my shoulder again. This time, I let her yank me back.

"No-go on the rear exit!" Zian called through the mic. "Two guards are watching and a third one's on the way! Find some other way out!"

"What other way?!" I asked my hacker buddy as Yukina kept us out of sight.

"Damned if I know, Bell, but whatever you can find, find it sharpish!"

I did some quick calculations in my head. Our primary exit was out, thanks to Mistake Number One. The front door was an even worse idea under the circumstances. That left the roof but we'd already cut the rope up there.

I remembered the rope Yukina used to get us inside. Putting my head next to my crime partner's ear, I whispered, "Run for the staircase. Don't stop until you're on the roof. I'll be right behind you."

"And what if you're not?" Yukina asked as a couple of flashlight beams got closer and closer to us.

"Then you use the goods we grabbed to save your uncle," I said, trying to sound more confident than I felt. "One way or another, I'll figure it out."

"You'd better," Yukina growled back before taking off for

the stairs at a dead run.

Naturally, this got the guards good and excited. All flashlight beams went straight to her like she was Lady Gaga on opening night. I yanked out my Sig from the small of my back, walked out of the doorway and fired four quick shots into the ceiling. Every flashlight beam fell off her like leaves from a tree in autumn—or the end of "not-winter", as we Cold City natives like to call it. Accompanying this lovely sight was the sound of a slew of bodies hitting the deck in case the next set of bullets came their way. That gave me enough of an opening to follow Yukina up the stairs.

I heard the distinctive grunts and slamming sounds of a fight as I got to the second-floor balcony, all of it coming from the right. I turned in time to see Yukina lay out yet another flashlight-wielding guard with her sheathed sword. The backpack made her a little less graceful than usual but not enough for it to matter. The fallen flashlight put a harsh glare on the beaten guard's face, who was moaning from the beatdown and the light in his eyes.

I saw more flashlights coming up the left staircase as Zian let us know, "Those guys on the bottom floor are coming up both staircases."

"Yeah, I can see that," I said as I fired off three more rounds into the ceiling. As expected, the guards hesitated and ducked for cover. I thanked my lucky stars—or at least the ones I had left—none of these guys were armed or this would have turned out a lot differently. A distinctive *thunk* made me turn back towards Yukina. She'd opened the door to the rooftop. After making sure everyone was staying put, I ran after her, grabbing the door before it closed shut again.

I took the stairs two at a time before coming back out on

the roof. As expected, Yukina took out her rope and was fixing the anchor to the edge.

She peered up at me as I got near her. "They won't stay cowed for long."

"So get to the bottom before they get here," I said to her, pointing at the ground.

She gave me a disgusted look that reminded me of Ramirez at her most annoyed. But she rappelled down the side of the building just the same. When the door opened a crack, I emptied the last of my clip into various spots around the roof. I heard some stumbles as our pursuers tried getting away from the gunfire. By the time my pistol clicked empty, Yukina had hit the bottom and was looking up at me.

I looked down at her and pointed towards the alley exit, nudging my head in the same direction for emphasis. She shook her head back at me and jabbed her own finger down at the ground. When I shook my head, she put her hands on her hips and tapped her foot while she glared.

"Nobody ever listens to me," I muttered in frustration as I went over the edge with the rope.

I heard the door open at last before I'd gotten more than a few feet down. This made me rappel a little faster.

"We got cop cars rolling up," Kennedy informed us. "I can't keep sitting here. What's your status?"

"Coming down off the roof, Spiderman-style," I said back. "Just start up the car and circle the block. We'll catch up with you in a bit."

"With this many units incoming?" Zian countered. "You'd better put a wriggle on before—"

I know he said some other stuff but I couldn't hear a thing. Three very sharp needles jabbed their way into my back and right shoulder. I'd enough time to figure out one of them had hit my recent bullet wound before I felt an electrical current roll through me like a freight train. I moaned and growled as my hands clenched on the rope, halting my progress. The second the electricity stopped coming, my fingers unclenched of their own accord and I fell off the rope. The good news was I pulled free of the needles. The bad news was I was still way too high off the ground to avoid injury.

I tilted back enough to see one of the guards holding something boxy in his hand over the edge of the roof. That's when I realized I'd committed Mistake Number Two. Sure, the guards hadn't had firearms but they'd made up for it with Tasers. *This is going to suck,* I thought to myself while I mentally braced for impact.

My landing turned out to be a lot softer than expected. I was relieved for all of two seconds before the smells hit my nose. "Oh, damn it," I muttered to myself as I picked myself back up off the trash heap I'd landed on. "Not again."

Lady McDeath's anti-death insurance had worked out with the usual mixed results. I came out of the open garbage bin I landed in without fatal or even serious injuries. But I now smelled like everything from banana peels to dust bunnies thanks to the slimy cushion I landed on.

Yukina grabbed my hand to help me out of the bin, but the way her nose wrinkled under the scarf, I knew she instantly regretted it. She raised an irritated eyebrow at me.

"Took the express elevator down," I quipped.

She shook her head in disgust before we both ran for the alley mouth. But up ahead was yet another unwelcome sight: the distinctive red and blue flash of prowling patrol cars.

12

GRAVE ERROR

"Somebody tell me some good news," I said into the earpiece, anxious at the sight of the incoming lights.

"The good news left the building 'bout the same time y'all did," Kennedy replied, concern and worry making her Texan accent heavy. "Just drove past three units and I can hear more of 'em are on the way."

"The front of the alley's clear for right now," Zian added. "But the nearest cop car is less than a block."

"Where are you, Candice?" Yukina asked, her voice concerned but controlled.

"A little over two blocks, honey," Kennedy replied with despair in her voice. "I could try to pull a Steve McQueen if you wanna but that might—"

A black sedan rolled up in front of the alleyway, screeching to a halt as the side door pulled up in front of us. Yukina and I stopped running; the unmistakable bulk of Kung, accompanied by two of his private security bodyguards in opposite facing seats, was waiting inside.

"Quickly!" Kung called out, waving us in.

"No, no, no, no," Zian yelled at me. "Don't even think—"

"Just track our exit, Z," I told my young friend, under my breath, as I ran for the door. "Kennedy, make a break for it."

"The hell I will, hoss," my reporter contact snarled. "You better tell me what they are getting into, Zian."

While everyone was talking, both me and Yukina climbed into the sedan. I grabbed the seat next to Kung while Yukina took the one facing him and me. The door closed behind us on its own while the driver smoothly pulled out. The engine made absolutely no sound and yet I could tell we were moving at standard cruise speed.

"Late model black sedan," Zian said into the earpiece. "Can't tell the make but it's moving up Spiros Avenue."

Doing my best to cover for having the earpiece, I looked a question at Kung while tilting my head towards the front.

"Electric engine," he explained. "In addition to being gentler on our fragile environment, it has the immeasurable benefit of running silent when engaged."

"Never knew those engines were tooled for sedans," I observed, giving the bodyguard between him and me a wary assessment. The bodyguard's face was as empty as the cases we raided.

Kung shrugged his bulky shoulders. "A custom job...And speaking of jobs, I do trust this unnecessary commotion outside comes with the benefit of the necessary requirements of yours?"

Yukina glared at him as she pulled down her scarf. "We have it."

She ripped open the lid's zipper, making the guard sitting next to her reach for his gun. Kung looked at him, shook his head and he held up his hand. Yukina ignored both of them as she gave Kung the bubble-wrapped statue. After pulling away the packaging, a smile spread on his fat lips.

Then he looked askance at the obvious bulk that remained inside the pack. "It would seem you spirited away rather more than what I requested."

Yukina's face went red before she looked at me. I nodded and she proceeded to pull out the other rare treasures we'd made off with. Kung's goons took on the task of carefully unwrapping these early Christmas presents for their boss. They were astounded by the antiques they found inside.

Kung himself was impressed. "I have to admit this is an unexpected development. Had you merely extracted the statue alone—"

"It would have drawn too much attention," Yukina finished. "But when one steals more than the actual target..."

It was stupid but I felt a swelling of fatherly pride at her words. She may not have believed them but she was smart enough to try and speak a language Kung could understand.

"Thus further muddying the trail that could conceivably lead back to either myself or Ms. Wada," Kung concluded, nodding his head. "Well spoken and reasoned, Ms. Tsing."

"Alright, we've got what you wanted," I said. "Is Mao off the hook now?"

Kung held up one of his stubby hands while the other one pulled out an ancient flip phone from his inside pocket. "If you'll permit me a moment...?"

I held back a snort but I nodded while my earpiece crackled to life. "Know you can't talk, hoss," Kennedy said. "But we got a lock on you. I'm about three car lengths right behind you."

"You've missed the police cordon they threw up about two minutes ago," Zian added. "Thing is...you're not heading back to Little Japan."

I glanced at the windows to verify this but they were so opaque I couldn't see anything. Meanwhile, Kung was talking in rapid-fire Japanese with Yukina listening closely. After a few seconds, my partner blew a relieved breath through her nose and shut her eyes.

"Don't matter," Kennedy said. "Wherever they're going, I can—"

I heard the distinctive squeal of brakes, making me wince. "Ahh, goddammit!" Kennedy snapped. "Some asswipe ran the light! I lost you!"

"Shit, you're getting away from traffic cams," Zian said in alarm, a few heartbeats later. "Bell, can you tell me... you...going..."

A wave of static kept chopping up Zian's words before finally fading out. Wherever we were, something was interfering with our ability to communicate. Cell coverage wasn't often an issue but there were still a few neighborhoods that were dead zones in this city. Maybe that could tell us where we were.

Kung sighed in frustration himself as he hung up the phone. "A shame that cell technology can sometimes lack the reliability of old-school phone lines."

Noticing my agitated look, he remarked, "Something the matter, Mr. Vale?"

I shrugged as casually as I could manage. "I don't know... Is there?"

"If you are referring to Ms. Tsing's uncle, the answer is no. While our talk was cut short due to a lack of cell signal, be assured my man is currently packing his things and leaving the scene."

I felt a lot of tension go out of my shoulders at this news.

"However," Kung added. "Since the both of you went above and beyond what this mission required, I do believe you have earned a token of my generosity."

I opened my mouth to request a lift home when I felt yet another needle jab into the side of my neck, complete with a steadying hand to make sure I couldn't pull away this time. I had enough time to see the goon nearest Yukina driving a hypodermic into her own throat before the world grew blurry. Two seconds later, it went from blurry to black.

———

Consciousness came back slowly. The first sign of it was a bitter chemical aftertaste that clung to my throat like seaweed. I cleared my larynx and shook my head to get it clear. That's when I realized I was laying on the ground... Moist, grassy ground.

I felt my foot bound to something, so I lifted my head to look over my chest. A severely worn-down gravestone stared back. "The hells?" I muttered as I gave it a firm tug.

It was a lost cause. My right foot was trapped, stuck to the grave by some metallic wire that held my ankle in place. I saw something blindingly white out of the corner of my right eye, making me look over. It was the tiger statue we'd gone to all the trouble to steal. I blinked as I thought I saw some sort of glow under its eyes.

I realized the source of the glow. A solid ring of white candles surrounded the grave I lay on, all lit with steady, hungry flames. It was a nice complement to the blue lines I saw going around me in a square pattern—energy flux, coming from the ley lines beneath our feet. The bird statue from the warehouse was to my right while the dragon one was standing behind the gravestone.

A glance over to my left helped me find Yukina. She was wide awake and struggling to get her own foot free from the bindings. I could make out the turtle statue behind her. A quick glance around the area outside the ring of candles, statues and blue lines told me where we were: the last spot in Cold City where anyone in the know about over the border business would want to be.

Yukina noticed I'd regained consciousness and said, "I'm starting to think you really suck at plans."

"Remind me to introduce you to my ex someday," I quipped to hide my uneasiness. "You two could compare notes."

But our Avenging Woman saw through me. "You obviously recognize this place. Where are we?"

"Pineshadow Cemetery," I told her. "Oldest official burial ground within the city limits...and the worst place in the world to pull what I think our captors are about to."

Yukina nodded as if that info helped her understand something. "That'd explain the heavy death vibes I'm feeling around us."

"Three hundred plus years of funerals will do that," I told her. "The last person put into the ground here was in 1967. But combine that with the ley lines intersecting under this spot and the whole area outside of it is a spiritual toxic waste dump." I realized this explained why our earpieces had stopped working, and why Zian wouldn't be able to locate us, no matter how hard he tried. "Every cell tower they've ever set up here has refused to work. Electronics break down after they've been out here a week."

There wasn't a thing I was seeing around me that refuted anything I was saying. Trees stretched their bare, weathered branches to the black night sky, as if ready to bring those limbs down on anyone who offended them. The other grave-stones littered the cemetery like unexploded landmines, mute sentinels to a world that had long since passed them by. Even the grass under us seemed yellow and sickly.

"And so it's the perfect place for the ceremony Zian found," Yukina concluded.

I was about to confirm her suspicion when I saw some-thing else behind the bird statue. In the late evening gloom, the peroxide blonde coif of Ms. Wada stood out like a warning flare. So did the small pack of Kung's men surrounding her, sweeping the area with their eyes and drawn pistols. While the latter had chosen their usual three-piece business suits, Ms. Wada opted for what I suspected was a bit more traditional wear. She sported a blood-red flowing kimono, a crimson flag in the midst of a sea of grey, black and yellow. Her imperious eyes fixed themselves upon us with a combination of hunger and hate. *Was this the part where she eats us?* a small voice wondered within my head.

Turning to the nearest man, she said something to him in Japanese. Yukina whispered to me, "She's telling him to get the rest of his men back beyond the perimeter until the cere-mony is over."

The man said something back that sounded like a protest. Wada cut him off with an angry stream of words which made him take a step back.

"He said—" Yukina whisper.

"Yeah, I got the gist of it," I told her.

Wada didn't stop staring daggers at Kung's flunky until he was out of her sight. Then and only then did she look down at us. She gave us a nicer look, disdain instead of outright hatred.

I shot her my cheekiest smile. "I don't think we've been properly introduced yet."

"I am well aware of who you are, Vale-*san*," Ms. Wada told me as she circled around us. She turned her eyes towards Yukina. "Just as I am aware Yukina-*chan* is the so-called *fukushuu onna*."

"This was Kung's plan all along, wasn't it?" Yukina asked, her voice barely holding back her anger. "Have us finish the statue set and serve us up as human sacrifices."

"Actually no. This ritual was to be performed on the land of my ancestors, but your incessant meddling has rather forced my hand. I suppose now this retched place will have to do."

She stopped walking and stood outside the ring of candles like she'd stepped out of that old music video by The Police. "Yours and Mr. Vale's interference in my affairs was both unexpected and unwelcome."

"Sorry, but I have this habit of trying to spot crazy women hell-bent on destroying the world," I said.

I noticed the blue lines on the ground were linked together in a solid square pattern. The flux of earth energies was solidifying and would soon be strong enough to power up whatever cuckoo spell she had brewing in her cauldron.

"You have no idea of what I want," she asked, looking all

but ready to swat at the annoying fly I was. "Tell me, private investigator. What do you know of me?"

I scrunched up my brain to remember what Yukina had said. "Rich family. Great job... Number three of your company, I believe?"

Her left eye twitched at my last words, and I swallowed nervously.

"And do you know who runs that company?" she asked, acerbic.

I could recognize a trick question when I heard one and remained silent.

"My father does. And do you know what will happen when he dies?"

I was no Einstein, but I could do the math. "You become number two?"

"Yes, while my brother becomes the new face of the company. And he can continue to drink himself stupid and fuck his whores—or is it the other way around—while *I* do all the work he takes credit for."

So that was what all this was about. "Look, sister, I'm all about gender equality, but don't you think this is pushing it too far? How about we call it a day, and I try to get you on Oprah or someth—"

I never got to finish that sentence. The tip of her high-heel pump landed square on the side of my mouth. The force of the impact toppled me and the taste of dirt mixed with blood.

A flow of Japanese rushed out of her lips, before she cooled down enough to return to English. "Even *gaijin* fools have their uses," she said, standing to her full height again.

"A sacrifice of blood is required to open the way and entice my queen to come forth."

I tugged on my shackle hopelessly as Ms. Wada did something more frightening than her usual menacing tone: she smiled. "I imagine two lives will truly whet her appetite."

13

SACRIFICE PLAY

A swirling black mass formed over the gravestone. I didn't need to stick my head inside of it to know what was on the other side: the Yomi section of Alternum Mundum—the Japanese underworld. *Yomi-no-kuni* is the Japanese word for the land of the dead, and the number one vacation spot for all non-living Shintô entities. Whoever Ms. Wada was summoning up, if we didn't do something soon, things were going to get very ugly for Cold City once again.

While I mentally reached out to the death energies around us, I told Ms. Wada, "Look, it's just us out here. Kung's guys are well out of earshot and you're planning on having us killed anyway. So what does it cost you to tell us the truth on this? Who's on the other side?"

I got a grasp on the ground's energies. I felt around until I could feel where the soil touched the wires stuck into it. If we were anywhere else, this trick from Lady McDeath wouldn't do either me or Yukina any good. But the current conditions were a perfect storm that I needed a little extra time to make work for us.

"I owe neither of you anything," Ms. Wada snapped, walking out of my field of vision.

I heard her footsteps stop above where Yukina and I were laid out. I had to do some contortions of my neck and back to see her upside-down. She stretched out her arms and began chanting. It sounded like it was in Japanese, but the pronunciation and accents were all wrong. It was more likely some ancient form of the language, or even a dead language that had a lot of similarities.

My muscles having hit their limit, I sagged back to the ground. I glanced over at our tiger statue in time to see its eyes *open*. Yes, I said "open", as in the invisible marble lids on them were slowing pulling back to reveal solid black orbs...of painite.

It was a good thing the precious gemstone was rare on this side of the border, because it had a knack for opening gateways between worlds. In the case of my bident, it opened the door between the living and the recently deceased. In the case of these statues, it opened up a portal to Yomi. Once the marble was out of the way, the painite revealed its true color, glowing red. The rift at our feet widened, foul whispers coming from between the worlds like suicidal thoughts.

The mark on my shoulder screamed in protest as it drew closer and strong gushes of energized wind hit me in the face.

All this gave me a big incentive to recheck the bonds on my feet. They were rusting, the energy beam eating away at it. If they were rope, they would have snapped already. As it stood, we still had a few seconds left before we could get free. I gave the portal a nervous glance as the noise from it grew louder and its mouth grew wider. I felt like I was trapped in a Poe story, as directed by H.P. Lovecraft.

Yukina hissed at me to get my attention. "Are you doing this?" she asked, nodding at her bond she was trying to break.

"Yeah," I said. "We should be free in another couple of seconds."

"And once we are, how do we handle this situation?"

Yeah, *that* would be the part I hadn't thought about. We could kill or knock out Ms. Wada, but that would still leave us with a partially-open portal through which a lot of nasty things could get out. And that was assuming her bodyguard detail didn't make short work of us before we could get much done. We were trapped.

"How much do you trust me right now?" I whispered back to her.

She tugged her feet, which came a bit loose from the ground. "You say that like I have better options."

"Look, no snark. For this to work, I need you to absolutely trust me here."

She raised an eyebrow at me. "So you have a plan?"

"Yeah," I told her, rationalizing that having part of a plan counted. "One you're not going to like."

"Is it as bad as your other plans?" she wanted to know, amused despite the life-or-death situation we were in.

"The worst one yet," I assured her with a smile. "If we're lucky, all we'll do is die."

Her eyes told me she'd made her peace with the idea of dying a long time ago. "Well...what are we waiting for?"

A set of metallic *tings* cut through Ms. Wada's chanting, making her stop.

"That," I said before rolling to my feet.

Ms. Wada resumed her chanting, as she motioned for her bodyguards to get back here. I could feel Yukina draw up beside me.

At our feet, the whispers turned into outraged moans that were near-deafening. But the only thing I was focused on was the portal itself. If Ms. Wada wanted a pair of human sacrifices, far be it for me to disappoint her.

Without a second thought, I leapt straight into the rift. Yukina, to her credit, did the same. The world darkened and the noises that assaulting my ears ceased the second we crossed the border.

14

DROP DEAD

Everything went black. Not in the "I got hit too hard in the head" sense but in the "my eyes weren't made for this much darkness" sense. All the air blowing up into my face told me I was still falling. But that was all I knew about what was going on.

My head knocked against something leafy and pliable. Having landed in enough of them, I made it out as a tree branch. More of them hit me everywhere...mouth, arms, shoulders, legs, chest. Even though some of them smacked me hard, not one of them stopped me from falling. I tried grabbing on but they kept slipping through my fingers.

I managed to get my arms in front of my head when I noticed I seemed to be slowing down. The branches were still coming but less and less quickly. Thankfully, they were also hitting a lot softer. Gradually, I felt myself come to a halt, right when my right hand touched the latest unseen blunt object.

"Vale?" I heard Yukina's voice call out to my left. It sounded a little muffled but clear.

"Right here," I said, moving my arm in and out to make sure my sudden lack of velocity had nothing to do with the branch in front of me.

"Why are we stopped?"

I looked around to see if I could find my traveling companion. No such luck...there wasn't enough light to see my hands, never mind her.

"Wish I knew," I admitted. "It's almost as if—"

Whatever I was going to say got interrupted by a spark of red light in front of me. A very distinctive sign formed from that light, a semi-circle sitting under a plus sign which itself was just below a full circle. I recognized it, of course. How could I not? I had it branded on my shoulder after all—Hades' mark.

Thanks to the lightshow, I was able to see Yukina beside me. She glanced at this sign with concern. "What is it?"

"Remember that someone I said you never wanted to meet?" I asked her.

When I saw her nod, I said, "I think she wants to have a little chat. Wish me luck."

I stretched out my fingers to the sign. When they touched the mark, I felt a shock run up my arm. It was like touching an electric fence...if the fence was charged with something uglier and less friendly than electricity. I felt the gravity turn back on and Yukina and I dropped again. I felt a few more branches slap me in the arms...

———

I was standing upright. I had no idea what my feet were planted on. A red circle of light surrounded me like a stage spotlight. Something told me moving out of it was a bad idea, so I stayed put. What I saw emerge from the blackness ahead of me confirmed my guess.

The first thing I made out was the red eyes. As those eyes got closer, the light I was under gradually showed off more of the owner's features. Even with the crimson rays on her face, I could tell her skin was deathly pale. But for the reflection from the light, the bob of black hair on her head nearly blended in with the shadows she stood in. The same went for the heavy suit of goth armor she wore, stylistically menacing in a Frank Frazetta kind of way. For some reason, she'd kept her short sword sheathed by her side. Given the anger I saw in those blood-red eyes, I figured it'd be pointing at my neck right now.

One thing I had to give Lady McDeath...no matter the circumstances, she sure knew how to make an entrance.

"What do you think you're doing, envoy?" she growled at me with her usual disdain mixed with anger.

"Your job," I quipped. "Last I checked, the Conclave is supposed to keep nasty portals from opening."

That line made her draw the sword. "You don't belong here."

"I wasn't planning on building a vacation home," I protested. "I wanted to avoid a repeat of what we put up with at a certain movie theater not so long ago."

She circled me to the left, her sword point aimed at my belly. "This place...it has no mercy for any man trapped within it."

"Yeah, I kind of got that impression," I said back, feeling

like something was off. "By the same token, it's likely also got no mercy for my side of the border if that rift ever opens up all the way."

I felt my boss' presence circle me like a shark waiting for its prey to bleed out. "Speaking of which," I continued. "Is the portal shut?"

"No," Lady McDeath replied as she came from behind my right shoulder. "Nor is it open. Both sides can glimpse the other realm but none can pass. You were *lucky* to have found a crack to safely slip through."

I blew out a sigh of relief. "Well, that's a start."

"You need to leave," she said, stopping in front of me. The sword point had stayed locked onto me the whole time. "Now."

That's when I finally put together what was different this time with her. "Love to but it's not like you've got a get-out-of-hell-free card to play. In fact, you're not even here, are you?"

The sword point penetrated the red spotlight to jab me in the stomach. I felt it dig into my flesh enough to draw some blood. "Care to test this hypothesis further?"

I nodded, surer than ever. "Yeah, right about now, you'd have done something to cut off my blood flow, make me choke, the usual 'I own you' power play. But instead, you're threatening me with a freaking *sword*? Those things stopped being impressive when we developed semi-decent firearms."

Her eyes flared but she yanked the sword back across to her side. Sheathing it made a hiss that felt like a credible death threat. She was in my head alright, and had decided to stop the mind games.

She backed her hiss with an inarticulate growl before

saying, "The ruler of Yomi and I are not on good terms. She has done everything in her power to keep my influence away from her territory." She pointed at me and finished with, "And you *will* be perceived as part of that influence."

The way she said it made me feel something I hadn't in a while: afraid for my life. What little I knew of Alternum Mundum, each individual realm had its own rules and conditions. While my side of the border was a neutral chessboard, the same rules wouldn't apply if the boss of a territory didn't approve of it. If Lady McDeath couldn't even come to this land to threaten me and had to rely on an astral projection beamed straight into my melon, then I feared I couldn't count on my death insurance working at all while I was here.

"I can bring you back, envoy," she said. The way she said it, it sounded like something she'd rather not do.

"Both of us?" I asked.

She raised an eyebrow. That got *me* angry. "Yukina Tsing...you know, my partner you yanked me away from? She qualify for your little evacuation plan too?"

She squinted at me. "What do you think?"

"That you're making a promise you can't keep or trying to get me to break my word. For the record, I'm not thrilled with either idea."

The look on her face told me she was even less thrilled by my words. That was one card I could always play with her. As her representative on Earth, my word was, for all effects and purposes, her word. And her breaking her word carried a lot of nasty penalties. So my giving my word to clients made her go along with a lot of things she didn't like.

"If you die here, you die alone," she told me. "And you will never leave."

"Tell me something I don't know," I said, letting my annoyance show. "Like how we can seal off the portal from this side of the great divide."

"Discover that for yourself," she spat before stalking back off into the darkness. Despite her stomping, her feet made no sound.

The red light around me faded out...

———

I hit the ground so hard, I felt it in my back molars. I let out a grunt, which turned into a total groan. Landing on all those branches had finally caught up to me. I felt like one giant bruise that couldn't even twitch, never mind move. Yukina grunted a bit herself but was quieter. I heard the rustle of her clothes as she got back to her feet.

Not wanting to be outdone, I shook my head clear and used my hands to push myself off the ground. My eyes had adjusted to my surroundings. There was light here but it was the dim glow of a solar eclipse or a sunset. It lit up the area like a barely functional fluorescent light.

While getting to my feet, I noticed the tall shoots of bamboo around us. Considering how sharp those could get, we were lucky not to have been impaled on our way down. All of them were an unhealthy dark brown, neither living nor dead. It was a match for the forest of trees around us, gigantic oaks and pines that towered over us like skyscrapers. In spite of the roughed-up condition they were in, the trees were still covered with enough leaves to totally blot out the sky. I saw no sun, no moon, no stars poking through them. As far as I could tell, the tree branches *were* the sky.

My landing had splattered a lot of mud on my face and neck. I took the time to wipe it off while Yukina walked over to me.

"Welcome to *Yomi-no-kuni*," she said in a quiet voice. She checked herself for her katana and didn't seem surprised to find it gone. "This is a bad place to be unarmed," she added.

I did a quick check of my own to find my Sig was gone from my shoulder holster. I tapped the inner ankle of my left leg and smiled. "I couldn't agree more."

I knelt down and pulled out my knife from the inner arch of my boot. The runes a djinn client of mine once put on the blade were burning bright. I held it up to her and said, "Always trust the idiots to miss something."

She gave me the smile back as she reached into and under her pants. I wasn't sure why she was doing that. This looked like a bad place for a striptease. But she kept messing around with her right pants leg until she finally pulled her hand back out. A set of throwing knives strapped to a nylon band came with it.

While she fastened the band onto her outer leg, I noticed something else that gave me pause. The source of the dim light around us turned out to be a light beam heading a good many clicks from where we were. It shot towards the nonexistent sky, pulsing between the trees. I thought I could hear a dim hum that kept perfect time with the pulse. Whatever Lady McDeath did threw us way off course. It was as if we were spat out of the beam halfway down.

Pointing at it, I said, "Want to make a bet that's coming from our way in?"

"I never bet against sure things," Yukina said, craning her

neck in its direction. "Ms. Wada will try again. How long do you think we have?"

"Hard to say," I admitted. "And not just because I don't know how quick she can get a backup sacrifice. No matter which part you wind up in, time moves differently on this side of the border. We could be here seconds and centuries could go by in our world. Or it could be the other way around. Only thing I know is we've managed to get ourselves a brief reprieve on her unleashing literal hell on Earth."

Yukina studied me carefully. "You've been here before?"

My mind flashed back to a sand-choked temple and a deadly duel I fought in it. "Well...not *here* here. But you do pick up a few things when you've been working the kind of cases I do."

"Is that how you knew going into the portal would be best?"

I winced a bit. "Don't hate me but it was kind of a lucky guess. I figured if there was no meal for our Scorned Woman, there was no reason for the portal to stay open."

She took a deep breath and nodded. "That's reasonable enough. Too bad it doesn't look like it was the right answer."

I tried my best to gauge the distance between us and the beam, but the thick foliage made that impossible. All I could say for sure was it was a lot further than a few feet away. "Let's head over there and see if we can find that right answer."

"Suits me," she agreed. "My nerve endings are telling me how unwelcome I am here."

"If it makes you feel better, so are mine," I told her as we walked.

But I didn't tell her everything. Even though the bad

vibes of Yomi were making me regret the lack of a fast exit, it was also setting off something else. Something about this place seemed...familiar. I could feel it churning from within the core of my being, which made no sense. Lady McDeath admitted she had no sway over this slice of Underworld. And she was the sum and total of all supernatural influence in my personal life. So why was being here feeling like coming home?

15

TORN AND FRAYED

After a little searching, we found a well-trodden path through the forest. The brown grass around it told me it hadn't been hard to create that track. Just apply lots of walking to the semi-dead grass. Both sides of the trail were lit up by ornate, covered lanterns that cast a pale light on it. The lanterns gave me the feeling we would have found it faster if the beam hadn't been alleviating the gloom. Once we figured out the trail wound in the direction we wanted to go, we followed it.

The one thing that got my attention about our surroundings was the stillness. In any other woods I've walked in, there was always something stirring or calling out. Sometimes, it was so loud you could barely hear your own footsteps over it. But here, you didn't hear crickets. It felt as much like a graveyard as the actual graveyard we'd come from...unless you counted the beam's hum.

As we walked under the roots of one tree that formed a

human-sized arch over the trail, Yukina asked, "So this someone I never want to meet...does she come from here?"

"Like I said, not *here* here," I told her, getting to the other side of the all-natural arch. "But she's from this side of the border."

"How did you two meet?"

I felt my jaw clench up at this innocent question. It's not a story I share often. "I wanted something more than was good for me," I said, forcing the words past the lump that had popped in my throat. "She gave it to me and it wasn't worth it."

The light of a lantern caught a troubled expression on Yukina's face. It made me wonder if she'd ever had similar feelings and conclusions about her vigilante work.

"Does she make you hurt people?" she asked, the trail leading us up a medium grade hill.

"Only the ones that deserve it," I told her, doing my best to keep my footing as we climbed. "Most of the time, the things I'm taking care of for her come from here. And it takes a lot to *really* hurt them before they do that to somebody else."

We'd reached the top of the hill by then. The beam looked a little closer but the foliage was still too thick to tell us how close.

Yukina took careful steps ahead of me on the downward slope. "So you were telling me the truth when you said you helped people."

If anything, that one hurt worse than the question about my getting involved with Lady McDeath. "I try, Yukina. I don't always succeed."

A sad, understanding smile came on her lips as she

glanced over her shoulder. "Neither do I. There's always people I can't reach in time."

"And it makes you second-guess yourself, doesn't it?" I asked, feeling myself warm up to my partner. "Could I have done this instead of that? Could I have been faster?"

Yukina grabbed my hand and gave it a squeeze. The movement was so sudden, I didn't have time to process it.

"I can see why Zian likes you," she said, letting my hand go. "You try to hide it but you really do care."

At the base of the hill was a shallow brook with clear water flowing over the rocks. In the real world, it'd have been loud enough for us to have to raise our voices. Here, I could barely hear the water go by when we were right on top of it. I took point as we got to the shore.

The water wasn't too deep and it had little current. The way it flowed over the rocks above its surface made me think slipping was a possibility.

"Best do this single file," Yukina offered.

I gingerly stepped onto the nearest rock. Once I was sure my foot was firmly anchored, I went onto the next one. I could hear Yukina taking that first step behind me.

"About what you said before," I pointed out, taking careful steps on the rest of the stones. "It's not all altruism. I do charge for my time so I can stay ahead of my bills, like anyone else."

"And have you ever met anyone else who did what you do?" Yukina asked, casually stepping on the stones as though it were carpet.

By this point, I was on the other side of the stream. I thought about her question as I waited for her to catch up. Once Yukina was by my side, we set off again

I answered her with, "No, not really. You might be the one who came the closest, though."

Her next question took me by surprise. "Do you consider me an idiot for not asking for money?"

I looked over at her in confusion. "Don't you already have a day job?"

"A day job where I'm constantly disrespected, chronically underpaid and have no room for career advancement," she all but spat. "I like being the Avenging Woman a lot better."

"Yeah, I can see why," I said. I'd certainly seen plenty of examples of that kind of sexism in the Navy. I did what I could to mitigate it but I was just one guy and never a CO, so my actions only had so much weight.

We stayed quiet as we kept walking the trail. Then she asked, "Is my uncle paying you anything?"

"No, this one's a favor," I told her.

Yukina hummed and took point on the trail. I had the good sense not to say anything else.

———

It seemed like those damn trees and bamboo would never thin out. But at long last, they did. I have no idea how long it took for us to get there. It could have been a few hours, could have been a few days. It wasn't like this place had many ways to mark the time.

I wish I could say what we found on the other side of those trees and bamboo shoots was a comfort. Sure, it was an ornate palace done in Japanese style laid out in front of us, overlooking a fairly tall hill. And maybe in the shadows, you could fool yourself into thinking it was something majestic. But the glare of the beam showed its pitch-black stone to have a jagged and sinister shape. It loomed over the landscape like the serrated edge of a knife blade. It was an artistic masterpiece the same way the literary output of the Marquis De Sade is considered classic literature.

The staircase going up to the oak gates had enough steps to give an Aztec pyramid a run for its money. At the top of them were a couple of guards standing so still I wondered if they were statues. They were flanked by a pair of uncovered torches that lit up the area a lot more than I was comfortable with.

From what I could make out, the beam was coming from the direct center of the castle. We were close enough to hear its hum clearly, like a computer on standby. I hoped for the sake of our side of the border that "standby" was still the portal's current status.

Yukina stepped off the path right before it went from dirt to stone. She circled the base of the hill from the left, quietly walking on the dirt and grass with nary a whisper. I once again marveled at how adept she was at stealth. She may have been a samurai by nature, but she was a ninja in her tactics. As if to underscore that last thought, she pulled up her scarf to place it over her nose and mouth. That gesture made me wish I still had my ski mask. I was tan enough for my skin not to stand out in the gloom, but it wasn't quite as good as Yukina's scarf.

We made a full circle of the hill. There were no guards on the walls but they looked way too high and sheer to scale. Likewise, nobody bothered patrolling the outer perimeter, which meant no one was looking for trouble. Still, Yukina found the darkest shadows for us to walk through. That suited me fine. The last thing we needed was to let them know we were here.

Just before we came back up on the path, Yukina held up a fist before making it an open hand again. She used that hand to pat the air towards the ground. Getting the hint, I knelt when she did.

Getting close to my ear, she whispered, "Did you see another way in?"

I shook my head. "Far as I can tell, front door is it. With all that torchlight around it, that's going to make getting in tricky if someone's watching."

She hummed and shook her head as well. "Assuming they're not statues, two guards...Take them out quietly and we could slip in unnoticed."

"Big if," I pointed out, holding up my knife. "We're down to knives and I'm pretty sure they've at least got swords."

"That's why we take them from behind," Yukina said before creeping up the hillside on her hands and knees. She kept herself as flat against the ground as her body would let her. This was one maneuver I could pull off as good as her. I said a silent thanks to my old drill instructor for putting me through hours of this kind of crawling as I snaked right behind her.

We eventually saw the guards themselves within the cone of the torchlight. A quick look at their ugly mugs almost made me wish I hadn't. Despite the fine armor they wore, they had uneven limbs, crooked fingers which looked like they could barely hold the swords in their hands and puckered lips they breathed loudly through. They resembled floating corpses pulled out of the water. I was sure I could have dunked both of them into the nearest torch without much of a fight.

Still, looks could be deceiving. If they were watching the front gate, chances were better than excellent they had ways to make our lives distinctly unpleasant. Yukina's plan was the safest approach.

Speaking of her, she put a hand on my left arm before turning her head towards me. Pointing at the left guard with her left hand, she pulled out one of her throwing knives with her right. She made a half-circle with her pointing finger before running it across her throat. Next she pointed at me, then the other guard, then my knife. I nodded and she slinked her way around the light's edge. As tempted as I was to get up on my hands and knees, I opted to crawl to get in the proper position.

The scent coming off my guy reinforced the corpse impression as I got close. His flesh smelled so rotten I wondered if I was about to do him a solid. I'd gotten to my knees when I spotted a bit of movement behind the other guard...Yukina. She raised her blade in readiness and I followed suit. She used her other hand to hold up three fingers...which became two fingers...and one. When she closed her fist, I moved.

My guy gurgled as my knife went straight through his windpipe. His body fell apart into a cloud of ashes. The sword he was holding nearly hit the stone before I caught it. It felt a lot heavier than a sword that short should have. His now-empty armor hit the soft ground in front of me. I looked over at Yukina to see the same scene had played out on her end. She was holding up the liberated sword with a critical eye.

Walking low over to her side of the path, I stopped next to my vigilante partner. She was startled enough to aim her knife at me before realizing who it was. Putting it down, she sheathed it in its leg holster. Sticking my own knife into the waistband at the small of my back, I tilted my head towards the gate and she nodded. I took point as we stepped inside.

The front yard had more sporadic torches than the path. They were scattered without any rhyme or reason about them, leaving most of the area bathed in deep shadows. A place this dark usually had people or creatures who didn't need much light to see by, but now the beam was lighting things up for those that did. I didn't know which part of that made me more nervous.

After doing a quick once-over of the area to be sure we were alone, Yukina used the available light to look down at her sword again.

"Something special about that one?" I whispered, my eyes doing its own sweeps to make sure we were still clear of danger.

"*Dotanuki*," she said like that word explained everything. When she saw it didn't, she continued with, "Heavy battle sword...Can take a lot of wear and tear before needing to be sharpened again."

I held up my own sword. "That's what this is too?"

She nodded. "They're both pristine. If we need to fight, they won't fail us."

I shot her a relieved grin. Good to know our situation had improved a little.

Then we heard a wheezing from the left side of the yard, followed by an inarticulate muttering. We searched around for a place to hide. Yukina yanked me towards a small bamboo grove. Granted, there weren't any better options that didn't require being out in the open, but that grove was so thin and porous, I knew we'd be spotted the second someone glanced our way.

The noisemaker stepped into the light of one of the random torches. She was dressed like a servant but this was no entranced bride or cute geisha. In both posture and skin quality, she looked like an old woman. And when I say old, I mean "walking through death's door" old. Her wrinkled face seemed to have been disfigured by a wild animal's claws. Her long white hair flowed behind her but kept leaving behind stray clumps in its wake. The same grave rot I'd spotted on the gate guard showed up on the parts of her body not covered by the robe. Her fingers tapered off into long, needle-point talons sharp enough to cut steel.

But the worst part was the sounds she was making. Unlike Ms. Wada's chanting, it didn't sound like a lost human language. It sounded like the senile ramblings of an old woman mixed with the death rattle of a fresh corpse. Every second of listening to it made me want it to stop.

The angle she was walking at put her squarely facing the grove. I tensed up for the inevitable alarm. But her ramblings never changed and soon she was hobbling her way towards the other end of the yard. Neither Yukina nor I budged until she was well out of sight...and hearing range.

"*Shikome*," Yukina hissed.

"Is it Japanese for 'extremely ugly old woman'?" I asked, trying to use my humor to mask my fear.

"That's close to the translation, *hai*."

I shivered. "Truth in advertising, that name." I frowned. "She should have seen us. I mean, we were right—"

"Her eyes may be in as bad a shape as the rest of her," Yukina offered.

"Maybe her ears too," I added with a nod. "All that muttering could have blocked out any sound we made."

Taking care not to bend the bamboo too much—who knows what else was listening—I pointed towards the portal. "This might also have something to do with it."

Yukina gave me a curious look.

"If they're used to a lot less light around here," I explained. "Something like that may be blinding them the way shadows do us."

"Why were the guards next to the torches?" she pointed out.

I thought about that for a second. "Intimidation...take a look at armed men like them and you might be rethinking whether going through the gate is a smart idea." I looked around the path again. "We should wait for her to come back around before—"

"Every second we wait is one we've lost forever," Yukina interjected while slipping out of the grove. "And she wasn't moving fast."

"Good point," I admitted while I followed her.

Soon, we were at the entrance to the interior section of the castle. No imposing oak door on this one; the way in consisted of a paper screen that slid back for Yukina with a hiss. A paper lantern hung inside, the dark wooden floors reflecting its dim light like distant fires. Putting her new sword a little ahead of her, my partner in crime scanned both ends of the hallway for trouble. When she gave me a nod, we both stepped inside. My boots made an unwelcome noise when they hit the floor. Both of us tensed up to see if anyone had heard that. I heard a distant groan coming from the right end of the hallway.

Deciding I needed to be a little quieter, I sat down to yank off my boots. Yukina hissed at me through her teeth, tilting her head towards the still-open door. I stopped playing with my laces long enough to tug it back in place. She angled her sword down towards a room that had some light coming from the other side of the paper screen. I just got my other boot off when we heard footsteps getting closer from the right. I'd tied my laces together so the boots could hang off my neck when Yukina grabbed me off the floor. She practically dragged me towards the room, using her sword tip to get the door open before pulling us both inside.

The lamp that was the source of the room's light was over the door, casting the rest of the room in some deep shadows. We both scrambled to get to the other end. Our own shadows went into hiding with us as we vanished into the dark.

The footsteps stopped in front of the door. I could make out a silhouette that was a rough match for the shape of the *shikome* outside. She raised her head to start sniffing the air. She hummed with a questioning note and sniffed some more. Yukina pulled out one of her throwing knives with her free hand before aiming it at the door. The monster gave out a bored "hmph" before walking back the way she came. The second her footsteps disappeared, I let out a sigh of relief. It took everything I had to keep quiet.

That relief lasted right up until I looked at the walls. The paintings hung there were a world away from the ones I'd seen at the museum. Though the drawing was elegant, they held no beauty, but rather overflowed with rage and horror.

I saw scenes of men being tortured by what I could only guess were demons...Specifically, female demons. A few *shikome* figured into one such tableau, gradually ripping bound men apart with their clawed hands while their prey screamed in agony. Another one showed men bound up in a giant spider's web. Everything but their terrified faces was cocooned while a thing with the torso of a woman and the lower body of a spider came down the web, presumably to feed.

Uneasiness gnawed at me as I realized how much I didn't belong here. If these old hags caught me, a fate worse than death was waiting for me. For once, it would seem Lady McDeath was truthful; this place really had no mercy for any man trapped within it.

The centerpiece of this macabre display was on the back wall we'd taken refuge next to. A picture showed a pack of *shikome* screaming in vain at a boulder that blocked off the cave they were trapped in. A man stood out in the sunlight, his hands pushing against the boulder and his face worried. Given what he'd gotten away from, I couldn't blame him.

Sitting near the left corner of this picture was some sort of shrine. From what I could tell in the dark, it consisted of lots of unlit candles surrounding a small, central plank of wood that stood on carved legs. There was Japanese writing on the plank but damned if I knew what it said.

While it disturbed me, Yukina appeared horrified at the sight. She swallowed hard and backed away from the shrine.

"What is it?" I asked, realizing this was the first time I'd ever seen her scared.

Her jaw tight, she pointed at the picture with her knife. "See the leader of the *shikome* pack?"

I had to squint into the darkness but I did indeed spot her. She was far more decayed than the others, a wild look on her skeletal features that all but broadcasted rage. She had her gnarled hands on the opposite side of the boulder, as if she were trying to push it open.

"That's our Scorned Woman?" I asked, a sinking feeling in my gut.

"Izanami-no-Mikoto," she breathed. "The Divine Mother and the reigning queen of Yomi."

"For real?" I asked, not quite believing it.

Yukina swallowed hard, before nodding. "These pictures... I believe we are in her castle." Tears sprang to her eyes, "I'm so sorry, Vale. I had no idea... I thought it was just some spirit, I never thought she would try to summon the Mother."

I knew better than to ask, but still..."Is it really that bad?"

Yukina's knife shifted its focus towards the man by the boulder. "That's her husband, Izanagi. And he would agree with you. He went down here to retrieve her. But he was horrified by what she had become since her death. He fled the scene. She followed him."

She gave another tense swallow before finishing. "By the time he dropped that boulder in front of her, she swore to take a thousand lives every day. He told her he'd create a thousand and five hundred in turn."

"Sounds like a dick-measuring contest," I muttered, marveling at the absurdity.

Yukina was anything but amused. "You joke because you don't understand. Before all this, they loved each other deeply. But their last child tore them apart."

Tuning into her wavelength, I tilted my chin at the wooden plank. "That's the child's name on the wood?"

She nodded as she lowered her knife to her side. "Kagu-tsuchi-no-kami, the spirit of fire. Izanami died giving birth to him. Izanagi beheaded him for the offense."

I recoiled. "But that was his son."

"Who killed his beloved wife," she answered, sheathing the knife. "We both know grief's rarely rational."

I nodded to myself, doing what I could to shake off the horror of what I was told. I focused on the lantern. "That may be why there's so many light sources around here. It's not for mood lighting. It's a tribute to Izanami's son."

Yukina tilted her head back in surprise. "Possible...Shikome don't need light to see by. And that kind of memorial makes sense."

I glanced quickly at the door before saying, "Sounds like it's more important than ever we close up that portal. I shudder to think what she'd do if she got out."

"A thousand lives a day wasn't boasting, Vale. She really has the power to cause this much destruction. Not to mention the shikome," Yukina said, padding her way to the door. "They'll gladly kill any living thing they can grab. Men especially."

She slid the screen back to peek her head out. Satisfied, she pulled it back and nodded at me. I followed her out of the room.

———

It took a little while to understand this part of the palace. The halls were laid out in a square pattern but none of the doors gave a hint of which one opened up to what. That led to a lot of empty rooms, dodging more *shikome* and hideous art exhibits which were anything but comforting to look at. One statue, in particular, stuck out: a man held down by chains while his legs were severed at the kneecaps by a demonic, sword-wielding female.

"I'm starting to think my coming here was a bad idea," I told Yukina at the sight.

"More than you know," she breathed. "No men are allowed here."

After touring several such rooms, we found a door that led us to the next corridor over. It was almost identical to the hallways we were in, but I could hear the hum of the beam on the other side. Maybe the next door over would get us there?

We wound up going through four sets of doors before we got close enough to see the beam on the other side of the walls. The lanterns made the beam's light less pronounced but there was no mistaking the sheer white tinge to it.

Yukina put her nose next to the wall and sniffed. "I can smell the outside air. The next door should be the last one."

"We could poke through this paper and go through," I proposed.

"Too careless," Yukina whispered back. "The *shikome* would spot it in an instant. Better to slip through the door. You can always close those behind you."

I was amazed by how practical she stayed after the shrine revelation. But then, how many times had I done the same thing while dealing with ugly ramifications I didn't see coming? There would be time to deal with all that later...if we lived.

That's when we heard a *shikome* moving around the corner behind us, which made the hair on the back of my neck rise. Yukina drew her sword just in case. I looked down the hallway for our exit, my eyes darting left and right. I saw it right in the middle of the hallway, the small gold knob the only one in sight. I tapped Yukina's shoulder before using my pointer to indicate the door.

The door was tied off with a thick cord to the frame to keep it from opening. The sound of Izanami's house demon was drawing closer and closer. Pulling out my own sword, I placed the heavy blade against the rope and sawed at it. Yukina kept the hallway ahead of us covered, her sword point aimed at the corner the *shikome* would round any second.

For all my efforts, the damn rope turned out to be a lot tougher than it seemed. The blade was cutting through but it was slow, grinding work. In a perverse way, it seemed like it was keeping pace with the demon hag's footsteps. Even as I rubbed the blade up and down more quickly, I wondered if I was too late.

I had about convinced myself we were done for when the rope gave way. I used the sword tip to slide open the door and tapped Yukina's shoulder twice before ducking outside. The rocks and dirt stung my feet but I did my best to ignore it. My samurai partner never once looked anywhere but the hallway as she backed out of the corridor and onto the dirt. Only then did she shut the door.

By that time, I'd had a good look at this inner courtyard. The portal stood in its center, the beam coming from it going all the way up into the nonexistent sky. A copse of ashen cherry blossoms surrounded it, along with a rough circle of dried chrysanthemum bushes. Altogether, they fashioned a garden that formed a barrier between the center and the paper walls around us. This place was like the rest of Yomi, caught somewhere between living and dead.

Beyond the *nature morte*, I saw the statues of chained, tortured men scattered as carelessly as the torches in the outer courtyard were. Their shadowy shapes appeared thin and wretched, as if a shipment of concentration camp victims was misplaced and sent here. They were maimed, their features distorted in silent agony. They sat in clusters ranging from four to seven, each cluster linked together by a chain that held them to the ground. I knew art was a subjective thing, but there wasn't a single thing I liked about these statues.

Doing my best to ignore the discomfort in my feet, I followed Yukina as we ducked behind the nearest tree. The cherry blossoms rustled a little as we hit the trunk, making some of the petals fall. As the door slid open, I wondered if that disturbance would be enough to give us away. The nearest cluster of statues next to it stood as an unpleasant reminder of what getting caught could mean.

Three separate sets of steady footsteps came into the yard, making Yukina and I scrunch further away from them. I decided my feet had suffered enough and moved to put my boots back on, listening to the footsteps as I did so. By the sound of it, they were all walking in the direction of the portal.

I risked a quick glance around the trunk. These *shikome* looked like they were in slightly better shape than the one we'd seen in the outer courtyard. They were still ugly and scarred up, but their flesh was less decayed and they moved at a decent walking speed. It made me wonder what had happened to the first *shikome* we saw.

That wasn't the only thing that was different. They were speaking to each other in clear Japanese. Yukina whispered into my ear, "They're wondering why the rope on the door was cut."

As I tensed, she added, "Relax...they're accusing each other of cutting it with their nails. The offender gets punished by their mistress. So they're dropping it."

Well, that was *some* comfort. But them not being there at all would have been a lot better. I finished tying my right shoe and slid back to my feet.

By then, they'd made it to the portal. The decaying women circled it, examining it from all angles. It gave me a chance to look at it myself. It was a dead ringer for the one in the graveyard, but it seemed to pulse awkwardly, like it had the gateway equivalent of erectile dysfunction. As the *shikome* continued to circle, I thought I saw the cemetery we'd come from inside it. But the image only lasted for a flicker of a second.

One of the hags said something to the rest in a voice that echoed across the courtyard. Yukina translated it as, "What is the meaning of this?"

Another hag spoke up and Yukina kept the audio subtitles going. "The Mother is being summoned. We should tell her immediately."

The third all but shrieked in dismay. "Have you forgotten what she did to Mariko for interrupting her prayers at the *ihai* of her most beloved son?"

"She should still be told," the second hag insisted.

"Told what? That a strange gateway has appeared in her

home and we have no idea where it leads? She would make you roam the outer grounds like Mariko for saying so little."

"It isn't going away," the second hag said. "And this noise, it won't stop."

It was reassuring to hear they hadn't tried to use it yet.

I heard a soft moan close by and I snapped my head around to find its source. Doing so, I nearly bumped against Yukina's head. The rest of the courtyard was empty. I couldn't see anything but us, the *shikome* and the statues. I looked a question at Yukina and she shook her head. She hadn't seen the source of it either.

Oblivious to the noise, the withered handmaidens kept talking. I got my head back in position for Yukina's translation. "Still, this is important," the third one said. "We should find out where it leads."

"Go ourselves, then?" the first hag asked in dismay.

"We have no better choices," the second hag asserted.

The moan came back with a vengeance. This time, I was able to pinpoint the source: the statues at our feet. Moving to stand by them, I knelt down and stared at the one closest to me. I waited and—there it was. The faintest of ripple beneath the skin in its left arm.

"What in all the hells," I muttered through clenched teeth. Dread filled me, as I realized how wrong I'd been to assume these were ever statues. They were actual men, more dead than alive...like everything else in this rotten place. Their clothes and the skin beneath was torn and decaying. Dust had settled on their unmoving limbs, giving the impression of rough greyish stone in the dim light.

They bore open wounds on their flesh that bled like coagulated car oil and barely seemed to have the strength to breathe. I couldn't fathom how much power it took for one of them to moan.

I looked more closely at the man facing me. He must have been close to my age, but it was hard to tell amidst the lines of pain that marred his face. His mouth was open in an eternal cry. But he'd long since run out of strength to scream.

Yukina moved to stand next to me, confusion showing on her face. "They shouldn't be here. Men are not allowed in the Divine Mother's palace."

"And yet here they are," I said, feeling a disgust rise through my throat which overrode my fear. It coiled into something darker and stronger. This was wrong on so many levels. How long had they been left to suffer like this? Neither living nor dying—an endless torture, always at a standstill. I didn't care who these men were or what they'd done to deserve this fate. I only knew it had to end.

Without further thought, I pulled out my sword and began chopping off heads. The blade barely had to break the skin before the bodies fell into dust. I'd sliced off my fourth when Yukina smacked my hands with the flat of her blade. The sword fell out of my grasp but it was too late.

The *shikome* had heard me and were staring right at us. A trio of nasty hisses was followed by them rushing at us with a speed I didn't think they had. I picked my sword up off the ground to get ready for the fight I'd stupidly provoked.

16

KNOCK DOWN, DRAG OUT

The Prime Directive of the detective game is "never assume". When you start doing so, you develop bad habits. For instance, you might think because one thing looks like another, both must be alike. Well, we call that a rookie mistake.

And I'd done just that. Because of their looks, I assumed *shikome* and old human women had a lot in common. When the hags threw themselves at me, claws at the ready, I realized how little the two had in common. Most little old ladies don't move like freight trains.

I'd barely raised my sword when Yukina rushed ahead of me, tossing a throwing knife at the one closer to her. While her target grunted and staggered back, my partner's heavy sword was raised high to deal some damage. Yukina swung at the leading *shikome*, starting with a pair of X-pattern cuts before finishing off with a slash aimed at her target's stomach. Those long nails on the hag turned out to be more than for show. She used them to deflect every one of my partner's blows, the meetings of steel against steel hard enough to leave sparks in their wake.

Undeterred, Yukina tried going for a deathblow with an overhead chop aimed at the *shikome*'s skull. Her Yomi-based opponent used both sets of nails to block it while one of her sisters made a swipe at Yukina's gut. The vigilante was agile enough to twist out of the way of the stomach swipe.

I may have been a little slower than her but I was doing anything but standing still. The *shikome* who'd taken that first knife was rearing back for an attack when I stepped in with my own version of a sword swing.

I had to admit my attack left a lot to be desired. Give me a knife or a gun and I can make it work, but I'm no Errol Flynn. My sword blow felt way off-balance, something not helped by the heavy blade I was swinging. So I wasn't surprised when the *shikome* batted my attack aside. But I *was* surprised by how much strength was in that block. It felt like hitting a piece of rebar with a baseball bat, and I took a step away.

I risked a glance at Yukina, who was being driven back by the other two. She was doing some blocking of her own to keep from being cut to ribbons.

I saw a flash of movement out of the corner of my eye. I ducked the claws of my own attacker while thrusting the sword straight into her chest. It struck home and I felt the satisfying sensation of the blade sliding in right next to the throwing knife. Not everything on her was as hard as the fingers, and the blade settled deep within her torso.

With a shriek, the decaying monster drew closer to me. She impaled herself further on the sword, as her clawed fingers reached for my face. I pushed her arms away with my free hand, and tried stopping the hilt of the blade ramming into me with the other.

Annoyed, the *shikome* reared back and gave me a hell of a headbutt. I saw an explosion of stars for a second before recovering enough to realize that I was toppling backwards. By the time I regained my footing, the *shikome* had pulled the sword free of her chest. She threw it off to the side before charging me again. Those stalactite claws were ready to do some impaling of their own.

I pulled my knife out before I sidestepped her swipes. I tried closing the distance between us but another swing of her claws made me jump back. I danced around her razor wire hands, trying to find a way in. Damn, but it was like going head-to-head with a pair of lawnmower blades. "Hells," I cursed, realizing she was too fast for me to not take a heavy hit in the process.

It took a lot to stay out of her way and I could feel my lungs burning. All that effort and I had nothing to show for it; even without hitting me, she was wearing me down. Sooner or later, this tactic was going to cost me the fight. The hag didn't mind toying with me; her shredded lips were stretched into a manic grin.

"Fine," I muttered between two breaths. "Time to play dirty."

I waited for the right swipe from her to get things started. I saw my chance when her left hand missed a swing at my chest. I switched my knife over to my left hand, thumb on the hilt. As I stepped forward, I jabbed the tip deep into the outer side of her wrist. She shrieked, more in annoyance than pain.

I kept running past her, the knife cutting its way from

the wrist to the bicep. Her scream rose an octave or two by the time I yanked the blade out.

Even with blood all over it, the writing on my enchanted knife still glowed like distant fires. I had no idea how much power the jinn magic carried into this realm. Hoping it could affect this thing like it did ghosts back home, I stabbed the hag right in the side.

She winced at the blow but didn't fall over. Confused, I pulled the blade out and stabbed her again. I got the same results. Before I could see if the third time was the charm, she pulled her wounded arm down, which trapped my hand under her armpit. With her uninjured arm, she took a swing at my head that I narrowly avoided. It wound up catching my shoulder, her claws doing the same shred number to it that I'd done to her arm.

Pulling back as much as I could, I let out a scream of my own, as blood ran down my bicep. The wound left me light-headed, and I remembered my death insurance policy didn't work in this place. If that *shikome* got the right blow in or I bled out, I would die, full stop, no takebacks.

A new feeling rose inside me, and I realized I hadn't felt the fear of dying in a long time. Sure, I didn't fancy getting hurt or losing a limb and always took great pain to give back as good as I got in a fight, but that primal instinct of self-preservation all living creatures possess from birth was put to bed when I became Death's envoy. Today, in this forsaken place, free of my patron's influence, it roared back to life with a vengeance.

I used my trapped arm as a lever to push the *shikome* away from me. No such luck; she stayed as rooted to the spot as any of the cherry blossom trees. I planted my left foot behind her right one and with a visceral scream, I pushed again. I poured all the strength I had, and the hag went flying over my hip and straight down. But the monstress held on tight and I went with her, winding up landing face-first in the dirt.

The hag rolled to her side and I could see the knife still in her chest. Forcing my brain to overlook my injuries, I stumbled over to her and threw a solid kick to the back of her head.

I reared back for another one, but keeping my balance slowed me down. It gave her enough time to roll back around to face me. My second kick was intercepted by the *shikome's* good arm. She yanked at my ankle and I crashed back to the ground with a groan.

I looked over my chest to see my opponent crawling towards me. "Oh no you don't," I muttered through a mix of saliva and dirt. I raised my right leg and gave her face another couple of kicks. Before I could pull back my leg for a third kick, her injured arm snagged my calf. With utter horror, I saw the long cut on her arm had about mended. I pulled back on my caught leg while I raised the other one.

"Will you just die already."

The push-pull effect did a lot to make my other foot hit her jaw like a Mack truck. She was stunned again, lying sprawled on the dirt a few inches away from me.

My eyes latched onto the knife hilt in her side. In one of the more reckless decisions I've ever made, I tried making a play for it with my bad arm. That gave her the chance to wrap both of her arms around me. Along with wrapping her legs around the back of my knees, she cut off any means of attack I had left. Letting go of my left leg, she thrust her hips forward, making both of us do a couple of barrel rolls to the right. On the third rotation, she used her arms and the momentum to throw me into the air. By the time I realized that I was sailing towards the tree I'd been hiding behind, I was two inches from impact.

I hit the trunk with a loud thump, my wounded shoulder catching the brunt of it. The bark cut into my many wounds all the way down. *Goddammit, I'm used to losing but this is ridiculous.* Talk about deceiving looks; nothing I'd done fazed the decaying old corpse of woman for more than a few seconds. And now she was running at me to finish the job. I forced myself to stand back up, using the tree at my back for support. The world started to blur at some point and the taste of copper had joined that of dirt on my tongue.

Behind the menacing *shikome*, I could see Yukina had resorted to using a tree of her own for cover. It looked like the only way she'd kept from being overwhelmed.

A familiar moan got my attention. It was one of the remaining wasted men I hadn't killed. Despite his pain, his eyes had a steady fire in them, like they'd been waiting for the chance to pay back his oppressors. My discarded sword lay right in front of him, smoking like it'd been dipped in lava or acid.

The moving corpse croaked out something in Japanese, pointing at the sword then the chain that still bound him. I didn't need Google Translate to get his meaning. I took a glance at our incoming mutual opponent. I couldn't think of a way to win this fight, but if I was going to die, the least I could do was do someone one last favor. "What the hells," I muttered, picking up the sword.

I used the last of my strength to bring the sword down on

the chain. The metal clanged as the blade bit deep into the link. Maybe it was the heavy blade, maybe it was whatever it'd pulled out of the *shikome*, but it only took two more strokes to cut through. In my peripheral vision, I saw the hag making a running slash at my neck. Despite the danger, my arms refused to move anymore, and I stood motionless like a deer caught in the headlight.

Something made a hollow thud as it got between her hands and my jugular.

I looked down to find it was a sword-length piece of bamboo, wielded by the living dead man I'd saved. Standing up looked like agony for him but those eyes didn't care. I don't know how many years he'd waited for this chance to get even, but there was little doubt he was going to make the most of it.

The *shikome* was as surprised as I was and she took a step back. She hissed her anger at the stranger, taking her eyes off me.

My arms found enough strength to lift the sword again. I swung it into the back of her nearest kneecap, yanking it back before it could get trapped like my knife.

The blow made her fall onto her back, where she turned her eyes onto me. Before she could move, the sharpened end of the bamboo stick went straight through the center of her neck. While she gasped her last breath, the man kept driving it into her like a stake through a vampire's heart. He pushed it in deep enough through her to sever her head from her body. Her arms and legs spasmed as her head rolled over to the base of the tree.

The effort made him lean against the bamboo to stay upright.

We had about three seconds of peace before Yukina came our way. Though she was somehow warding off the other two *shikome*, her own exhaustion was plain to see. Her dark hair was matted with sweat, gluing strands haphazardly across her reddened cheeks. By the looks of it, she wasn't going to last much longer either.

The only edge me or my new comrade had was neither of those hags had seen us yet. I leaned against the tree to get back on my feet while my rescuer tugged out his bamboo stick. I wound up getting as far as my knees while he tugged his stick loose.

The hag on the right was making a play for Yukina's rib cage when he intercepted it with his improvised weapon. The monster seemed shocked by this turn of events, enough to stop fighting. She looked enraged when she realized who blocked her. She broke off from Yukina so she could start striking at him. Despite the fact her hands were a blur, he managed to put the bamboo between him and every blow she tried. Where he found the strength to keep it up, I had no idea.

Yukina herself seemed to get a second wind from having the pressure of an additional attacker taken off. But I knew our new friend had only bought her an extra few seconds. A repeat performance by yours truly looked to be in order.

Taking a deep breath, I crawled over to my partner, sword in my right hand. I'd have used my teeth to carry my weapon if the blade wasn't smoking from whatever was on it. I hugged the ground as tightly as I could to stay out of the way of both their blows and didn't stop moving until I was behind the *shikome*.

Rolling onto my back, I thrust the tip straight into her

lower back. I don't know if it came out the other side but I felt it go in deep. The thrust stunned her enough to make her lean back and assume a T-pose.

That was all the opening Yukina needed. A second later, a metal blur made the *shikome's* head and shoulders part company. I yanked my blade back out, rolled over to the right and let the corpse fall to the ground next to me.

Yukina leaned against the nearest tree, panting heavily. Our freed captive was thrown into her and I rolled over to see if I had to defend my companions, but the last surviving *shikome* decided she'd had enough. She fled the scene, throwing the nearest door aside to make her escape.

Unless I missed my guess, she was deciding, wrath or not, the time had come to wake up the Divine Mother. And none of us needed to be here when they returned.

17

LAST STAND

Sheer willpower was the only thing holding our walking dead man up. With the fight over, he collapsed in utter exhaustion; whatever strength he had was now spent. His head wound up facing me, so I took that opportunity to tell him the only real Japanese I knew: "*Dommo arrigato.*"

His eyes went from fiery to glassy. I had no clue if he'd heard what I said. Worse yet, saying those words took the last of my strength too. I leaned my head back on the ground, wanting to sleep. I fought the impulse. I knew if I fell asleep now, I'd never wake up. But I'd lost too much blood...fought too hard. The adrenaline left me; it took me as far as it could and I was left feeling hollow.

I spared a thought for Lady McDeath and her last words to me. The mark on my shoulder, *her* mark, was silent. For the first time in years, I was alone.

"If you die here... you stay here," I muttered to the ground beside me, "and become one of those living dead statues."

Despite her own lack of strength, Yukina was dragging our new friend's body to the portal. I doubt she was thinking of leaving me behind, but he was in worse shape than either of us. If anything could be done for him, now was the time.

"Alright," I wheezed out. "Nap time's over." I used the arm that still worked to push myself off the ground. It took several tries and grunts to get to my knees. When that went okay, I picked myself up the rest of the way with the help of the tree trunk. The world swayed and swirled around me and I came dangerously close to kissing the nearest flowerbed.

Yukina had stopped dragging the man and was standing right in front of the portal. Her eyes glued to something at its base. I ambled over to her on shaking legs. I glanced down and found the source of her confusion. The portal wasn't on the ground. It was floating above a small, glowing pool of water. At least, I assumed it was water.

The pond was surrounded by small round-shaped rocks that were meticulously placed to surround the crevasse. The liquid inside was clear and rippled like water did, but a couple of details—aside from the glowing—left me dubious as to its true nature.

The surface was moving without any discernable reason; it seemed to be churning as if it had a will of its own. It was almost like a pulse, beating to the constant hum of the beam we'd been hearing all along. Something else ebbed out of that water. I could feel it deep in my bones, something more primal, a dark energy of some kind. Putting the pieces together, I had to conclude this was a vital part of what was powering the portal.

Yukina noticed me, startled. "Are you—"

"Still...breathing," I had to force the words out. "Need to...help...him."

As I moved forward, she put an arm in front of me, stopping me and steadying me at the same time. "He told me he had to do this himself. Let's honor his wish."

I didn't have the heart to question her. I backed off, letting her take much of my weight as we waited. Whoever this man was, he'd more than earned that much respect.

Even so, he was trying to reach the edge of the pond but couldn't do more than twitch his fingers. He managed to stretch his arm out to the edge and the water stirred harder. Within seconds, it was practically bubbling.

Yukina took a few steps back and I went with the motion.

We watched in amazement as tendrils of water leapt out of the pond, forming into a delicate hand. It took the man's own and a soft voice murmured, "Now is not your time, husband."

I was still puzzling why I was hearing English when the hand morphed into a solid sleeve of water that ran up his arm. It rushed into his mouth and he gulped it down like a dehydrated man who'd stumbled upon an oasis...which wasn't far from the truth.

With each gulp, his flesh filled out. His skin went from desiccated to wrinkled to supple. His muscles reassembled themselves, swelling with the kind of power and build that comes from a lifetime of intense activity. His face went from mummy to Japanese Prince Charming, a perfect complement to his restored and darkening shoulder-length jet black hair.

He sighed as he said, "I never deserved you, my wife," before standing up. His rags practically fell off his body.

Only his loincloth seemed to hold together, a dirty white pair of strips containing his privates and coming together as a thong in his butt. Turning to face us, he caught my gaze and held out his hand. "May I borrow your sword, please?"

I had enough presence of mind to hand it to him. "Hope you get better use out of it than I did."

"I will," he assured me before walking away from us. Maybe it was the shock of the last few minutes compounding on me, but it took a second for me to realize what he was about to do. The next second, he cried out as he struck down the other men in chains, finishing the work I started.

Wanting to focus on anything but what was happening, I pointed at the pond. "What is that, Yukina?"

"I'm not sure... I think..." She swallowed, before averting her gaze. Her face was taut, and a white shade of pale. "I think it's a pool of souls. The old stories speak of it. In life, the souls' owners were tortured and every indignity they endured led to another drop in the pond."

Whatever reply I could offer was trapped by the lump that surged in my throat. This explained the state of the prisoners, not just caught between life and death, but kept there on purpose. Their tormenters were drawing out their torture to keep the pond fed. Day after day, drop by drop.

When Yukina looked at the water surface again, it was with a sneer. "It's nectar to the Divine Mother. She bathes in it to restore her youth."

I looked away. The more I heard about this goddess of the underworld, the more I understood why her ex left her to rot down here.

The battle cries of our restored friend ceased and a sudden breeze stirred. I turned in time to see it lift up all the ashes of the fallen from the ground, turning them into separate clouds of dust that floated like an aggressive bee swarm.

"Brothers," the man said. "I have no right to ask this of you, any of you. But if you could defy our captors one last time, I swear you shall be avenged."

The dust clouds went haywire, flying around in a frenzy. I wasn't sure if that was a good sign. In an instant, all of the dust splattered itself against the door and walls of the rest of the castle. The bee metaphor kept rolling through my head as I heard the angry buzzing from the dust particles. I had a feeling it was going to be a lot tougher for the *shikome* to come back in than it was to leave.

The man came back to us, his face full of the same resolve I'd first spotted in his eyes. "Misa Asao, sworn companion of Shiro Amakusa," he told us, holding the sword out for me.

I held up my hand and shook my head. I'd meant what I said about him getting better use out of it.

"Tsing Yukina," Yukina answered. "Sworn protector of Little Japan."

"Vale Bellamy," I answered, getting the pattern of the answers. "Very confused private investigator."

Taking the sword back, Asao looked at me with some amusement. "And what confuses you, Vale-*san*?"

"How you're speaking English, for starters," I pointed out.

He shrugged. "I am not. I am speaking the language of spirits, which needs no translation." He turned to Yukina and gave her a deep formal bow. "I am honored to meet you, Tsing-*sama*. Your family's swords are much prized by my class."

"You were a samurai?" Yukina asked, not looking surprised for the first time.

"Ronin," he corrected her. "But, as I am sure you know, every samurai eventually becomes one."

She smiled at him. "Seven times down, eight times up."

"Indeed," Asao said, finishing his bow. "In my case, I merely had six masters in my lifetime."

"Speaking of up," I interjected. "How long can our dead friends keep the lady of the castle at bay?"

"Not very long," Asao admitted, his eyes assessing the situation. "But long enough for me to tell you what you need to hear."

"Like how to close the portal from this side?" Yukina asked, her eagerness evident in her voice.

Asao shook his head in sorrow. "Alas, Tsing-*sama*, the only way to seal this breach is from the other side. The pool of souls ensures that much."

I heard thuds on the other side of the paper walls. The walls and the dust on them held but Asao hadn't been wrong about this lasting only so long.

"Why did your wife wind up in this pond?" I asked him.

Shame stole over his stoic features. "She was my ghost bride. We had planned to be married in a Christian ceremony after the fall of Hondo Castle."

"So you're a Christian?" Yukina asked in surprise.

"She was. I was not. But I had a duty to her I did my best to uphold. When we failed to take Hondo, the shogunate forced us to retreat to Hara Castle. Before we reached it, I sent her home to her family."

"And they *were* Christian?"

Asao shook his head, tousling his straight hair. "The

Jesuits had never converted them. And they had disowned her for her new faith. It was still safer than being with us."

The walls shuddered again. The dust came loose for a second before reattaching itself back to its post.

"Okay, how does that explain how did you both wound up here?" I asked.

"The Dutch cannon proved to be my doom at Hara," he explained. "Mariko's parents had my body smuggled out of the castle. They punished her by making her my ghost bride, in a traditional ceremony."

A twinge of hate shone in his eyes as he went on. "They married her to my corpse before forcing her into the earth with me. She died in terror and pain and there was nothing I could do but feel outrage. My outrage and her death was enough to pull us both into Yomi. And I have been trapped between life and death for who knows how long."

Yukina hesitated before saying, "It's been nearly four hundred years."

Asao took that in stride. "Did our rebellion succeed?"

She gave him a solemn shake of her head. "No."

This time, the shuddering walls made the dust a little harder to come back from. Time was running out.

"Look," I said. "As fascinating as all this ancient history is, we've got another couple of blows left before they break through. Do you know how to slam this gateway shut?"

"Destroy the Guardians, destroy the link," he said, pointing his sword in the direction of our exit. "Nothing else will suffice."

"But how do we—"

I stopped talking when I saw the inner darkness of the portal clear to show the grave. The image was too distorted to see if anyone was there but I doubted anyone would be crazy enough to come over.

"I have a feeling Kung and his men might object to that," Yukina said, nodding at the portal.

"All truly worthwhile goals have great difficulties, Tsing-*sama*," Asao answered, assuming a fighting stance. "And there is no one else but the both of you to accomplish this."

I turned to him, startled. The young man shook his head at my unspoken question. "I am still dying, Vale-*san*. Nothing can stop that."

I almost told him to take another drink from the pool if he needed a boost. Then, I remembered what the pool was made of and felt ashamed of myself.

"You seem very healthy for a dead man," Yukina argued, not wanting to believe it either.

Asao held up his right arm to the pool and beam's mutual light. Water still glistened off his skin, but it was drying up. "My dear wife has only given me partial strength. Even had I drank the whole pool dry, it would still not be enough." He sighed, and it came out sounding resigned. "Too much time has passed, this body is become the mere husk of a fractured soul."

The walls banged and I could hear the shrieks of the *shikome* come through the other side. Some of the dust fell back on the ground, never to rise again. I looked at Yukina and at the portal; we had to hurry if we wanted to escape *Yomi* with all of our limbs attached.

I turned back to face Asao. The injustice of the situation made me grab his shoulder and say something I hadn't said since my family died. "This isn't fair."

I was startled by the tears I was blinking back. Yukina grabbed his other shoulder with tears in her own eyes.

He looked between us with a touched expression. "Do not grieve for me. It is only because of you I shall die the honorable death I was denied for so long. And I shall do so by taking as many of our foes as I can while defending your retreat."

I let go of his shoulder and whispered, "You deserved better, man."

Yukina did the same and she stalked closer to the light beam. As we marched to the gateway, her expression grew thoughtful. A small frown tugged the right corner of her lips as she glanced at the pool.

"We need to go," I told her, dreading what she might be thinking. "They're going to bust through any second, and the cemetery is going to be their next stop."

Her eyes went from looking at the water to me. "Go on ahead. There's one last thing I can do to help us out."

That got me alarmed. "Don't think of—"

"I swear on my family name, I'll be right behind you," she told me, putting her hand on my shoulder. "But let me do this, Vale. It may mean the difference between our success and failure."

I was trying to think of a snarky comment when the wall gave way. The *shikome* on the other side of it were held back by the dust, but not for much longer.

Growling my frustration, I leapt into the portal and hoped to hell Yukina meant what she said.

18

HEADS UP

I wish I could say the way back out was less painful than the way in, but that kind of luck only happens in badly written fantasy novels. Did I go into the actual portal in the garden or did I go through a wind tunnel that was sucking me into the portal proper? Night swallowed me whole and I realized that was a question I'd never get the answer to.

I was spat back out onto mushy ground, giving me one last blow to try to shake off the pain. A quick glance up at the trees, the graves, and the actual night sky showed me I was back in Pineshadow Cemetery. The first drops of an incoming rain shower fell on my head.

I moaned as I propped myself up on my elbows. Something thrummed within me, and I recognized the feeling right away. The tattoo etched into the skin of my right shoulder sang with it, letting me know I was back under my boss's influence. And not a minute too soon, I could see. The ley-line powered energy flux that surrounded me was as tangible as a laser. Gone were the intense variations and hazy flickers. The portal leaping close to my feet was steady and bright, signaling the gates to Yomi were wide open.

I reached for the nearest gravestone and used it to get back to my feet. Ms. Wada stared at me from the other side. Anger was quick to replace the surprise on her face. She was still clad in the robes from earlier but was now holding a black umbrella to ward off the falling rain. Her eyes blazed with the kind of hatred I usually associated with Lady McDeath...and I'd rather have been staring at the latter instead of the former right then.

By her right side was a surprise...Kung. The big man held up a black umbrella of his own. Those chilly eyes of his didn't have any hatred to throw. They looked annoyed more than anything, as if there were better things he could be doing with his time right now. He gave the impression of a reluctant family member who'd been dragged to a distant relative's funeral.

Ringed around the grave were a lot of hard-looking men dressed in matching three-piece suits. Given they had the kind of numbers to cover this place's perimeter, I could only presume this was the bunch Ms. Wada had called up when Yukina and I bolted. No umbrellas for these human pit bulls...The only things in their hands were guns ranging from semi-autos to SMGs. All of them were aimed at my head.

"All this...for me?" I asked, mustering up a smile. "You shouldn't have."

"A slight correction, Mr. Vale," Kung said in a tight voice, sounding anything but amused. "We shouldn't have to."

I let a little chuckle spill out. "Touché. Ah well." I

shrugged and pain shot through the still-bleeding cuts. "It's the thought that counts."

Ms. Wada strode up to me, disdain palpable in every step. "Where is the girl?"

I glanced up at her. "Could you be a little more spe—"

When my head cleared again, I felt a new bruise forming on my left cheek and saw Ms. Wada setting her right foot back on the ground. That's when I saw that something about a grave outside the perimeter didn't make any sense. Before I could process it, I heard the scrape of metal against leather over my head. From under her sleeve, Wada pulled out a small but sharp-looking dagger.

As she crouched down on her haunches, she let go of her umbrella so she could run her fingers through my scalp. Tightening her grip on my hair, she pushed my head back so my face was left catching raindrops. When she aimed the dagger tip directly at my right eye, I didn't dare blink the water away. "I will not ask again, *gaijin*."

As disturbing as it was to have a sharp piece of metal that close to my face, it did give me an important reminder. I'd left my own knife stuck in the side of a dead *shikome* back in Yomi. And it was a certainty that Ms. Wada wasn't about to let me borrow hers.

Despite being unarmed, I couldn't resist mouthing off. "Her flight got delayed. She promised she'd catch the next one out."

I mean, that was kind of close to the truth. I hoped Yukina would keep her promise, as this party was short on friendly company.

"And the Mother?" she went on, bringing the knife far too close for comfort. "Where is she?"

"Funny thing," I said. "Her secretaries—you know, the wrinkly ones who look like they need hourly Oil of Olay baths—they said something about her taking an extended nap they didn't want to disturb. You should try to book an appointment next time."

I was amazed she let me finish that smartass reply. But the expression on her face told me I was about to pay for it. *Biocular vision was fun while it lasted*, I thought as she pulled the knife back to stab.

"With respect, Ms. Wada," Kung's voice cut in behind her. "I believe Mr. Vale is deliberately baiting you. I recall he did so quite a bit when we first met."

Ms. Wada turned to face him, the knife still poised to strike.

"While he seems to be doing this for his own amusement," Kung went on, sensing he had an opening. "I can only assume he is also doing so to enact some stratagem at the moment you lose sufficient control. If I am correct, it would likely be a waste of your time to play his game, true?"

Even though she scrunched up her face, the fire went out of her eyes. She growled at me one more time before throwing my head back as she let go of my hair. I didn't mind the rough treatment. At least now I could blink away the water in my eyes.

The knife went back under her sleeve as she grabbed the umbrella and stood back up. "I have to admit that was well-reasoned, Kung," she said, her voice dripping with begrudging respect. "In fact, that is possibly the first sensible thing I have heard you say since this affair started. After all, I still need food to feed my mistress."

As she turned around to walk back to the portal's edge, I

saw something out of the corner of my eye. A snap of blonde hair was darting between the trees on my right, over Kung's left shoulder. Since everyone was focusing on me and the giant portal to hell, I was the only one who seemed to notice.

The blonde head poking its way around the tree left no doubt on its owner: Kennedy. Even in a techno-dead zone like here, it was only a matter of time before she and Zian tracked us down. Still, for this to work, I needed her timing and placement to be right.

I took a second to pretend to look over my whole grave-side audience. What I was doing was searching for a safe spot for Kennedy to come in at. I moved my left shoulder in what could have been a shrug that also happened to point at a stout tree directly behind the leftmost guard's back. Kennedy nodded and faded back behind the trunk.

"So," I said, raising my voice to be heard by everyone. "All that to get back at your brother, heh? I mean, I get it. Daddy likes him best and that sucks. But—"

Ms. Wada turned on her heel, the knife back in her hand.

"—don't you think this is taking it too far. I mean, summoning an evil goddess on Earth, what do you think this will accomplish? How many innocent women will you crush beneath your boot while you're on your way to the throne?"

"You are a worthy representative of your gender, Bellamy Vale," she snapped, her voice ice cold. "All silver tongue and charming smiles. Men such as you should be put on a leash, their tongues cut off." I swallowed hard at her words. "My queen has languished in Yomi long enough. Banished for a crime she did not commit, cast away because *a man* could not keep his word. No more. Tonight she will return home and the tide will turn."

Flashes of light illuminated the entire cemetery as the portal pulsed harder and something was hurled out of it. Yukina landed a few feet to my right, with a moan of her own.

After a short moment of surprise, half of Kung's men took aim at her. The others kept the muzzles of their semi-auto pointing at me. I didn't know where he'd acquired his security detail from, but these guys were good. I knew plenty of tough veteran-turned-private security who'd have long-since run away in front of such weirdness, but Kung's men weren't fazed by the supernatural. I shuddered to think what else they'd seen to be so jaded.

All the commotion gave Kennedy the opening she needed to get into position. I saw the silver flash of a gun in her hands before she disappeared behind the appropriate tree trunk.

Kung spat out something in Japanese at the dramatic entrance of Yukina, taking a couple of steps back. By contrast, Ms. Wada looked as though she were ready to plunge her knife directly into the young woman's throat.

"Glad you could make it, partner," I told her as she raised her head. Underneath the wild strands of black and red hair, her face was pale and tired. But her resolve shone bright in her almond-shaped eyes.

The heavy sword she'd been using on the other side was in her right hand, but I doubted it'd do much against bullets.

To her credit, Ms. Wada settled down and gave Yukina a confident smirk. "And now, we shall finish what was begun earlier."

"Hey, quick question," I said, turning towards Yukina. "What did Kung say just now?"

"That was a Buddhist prayer," she said, as her eyes burned. "A call for mercy in the next life."

I was about to comment on that, but a thought caught the words dead in my throat. There was something wrong with Yukina. The vigilante was getting back to her feet and I looked at her closely, but could not place it. Something about her voice—hell, her mannerisms—was off-kilter.

Before I had time to ask her if she was alright, I saw Kennedy poke her head around the trunk. I glanced at her and frowned with the left side of my face. She got the hint and backed off.

"Planning on burying us here like you did the ghost brides?" I asked Kung. There wasn't any reason to ask that. Kennedy was ready to go. Yukina would likely leap into action the second things kicked off. But I had too much curiosity to leave certain questions unanswered, and I needed some extra time to get my thoughts in order.

"You will be past caring when you are dead," Kung spat. He still looked unsure of himself, and there was little doubt he was wished hard he was somewhere else.

"A pity your victims didn't get the same courtesy," Yukina answered. "Their souls trapped for so many moons in the dark realm."

This time, my frown was genuine. Despite her Japanese background, Yukina had no accent when she spoke English. But now, there was one. It wasn't as thick as Ms. Wada's, but the faint traces of an out of town lilt clung to her vowels.

"You put them in this ground and let them die in it," she went on, pointing her chin at the very grave I noticed, "and thought nothing more of it, but what of the torment that followed? The torture bestowed upon these innocent souls for the rest of eternity?"

Ms. Wada muttering in Japanese some nasty-sounding stuff I'm kind of glad I didn't understand. Kung gave me a shrewd look and said, "That is beside the point. As you have correctly guessed, you are about to join them there." He raised his hand, a signal to his men to open fire on us.

"Won't shooting us counter the ritual?" I rushed the words out.

"At this point, only the death itself matters," Ms. Wada explained through clenched teeth. "Now if the both of you are done with your questions, it's time for you to face it."

"*Wakatta*," Yukina said, lowering her head as if in surrender. She cut her eyes over to me and gave a subtle tilt towards the ground she was lowering her face towards. I followed her example with my own head.

Kung was barking orders when I whispered, "Please tell me there's a plan here."

She gave me a smile that didn't belong on her face. "Seven times down, eight times up."

I barely had time to think of the implications before she moved. And when I say "moved", I mean moved so fast I had a hard time tracking her with my eyes. Two silver blurs cut through the rain-soaked air to hit their targets: Kung's raised hand and Ms. Wada's shoulder. A split-second later, a pair of loud booms split the night, knocking down the hitter right next to Kung.

While Kennedy ducked back behind her tree with a smoking gun in hand, Yukina rolled to her feet. Three more throwing knives caught the suits on the right on the way up.

She tossed something at me as she went for the nearest gunman. My mind barely registered it was my knife before she ran her thick sword through her opponent's guts and ducked behind him for cover.

The sudden movements made the gunmen on the left panic. They fired across the graves, making me hug the ground for all it was worth as my left hand snatched the knife from the dirt. The only thing the hail of bullets hit were the three wounded guys Yukina used for a dartboard.

The vigilante darted around the shots like she was skipping across the street, winding up at Ms. Wada's side. The tall blonde swung her umbrella at Yukina long enough to get some distance between them, her dagger held menacingly in her deft fingers.

Meanwhile, Kung recovered enough to bark out orders that made most of his men fall back for cover. He dropped his own umbrella while backpedaling from the danger zone, the better to clutch at his wounded hand.

Still, one of the guards had the bright idea to run right at Yukina, yelling at the top of his lungs with a familiar sword raised over his head. Her eyes widened in fury as she met his charge. Using her lack of height to her advantage, she let herself fall on one knee and used the momentum and the muddy rain-soaked ground to glide the remaining distance. The man's blade swung through the air above Yukina's head, while she thrust her own sword under and through his chin. While he gurgled his last, she let go of her borrowed sword to take back her rightful property as it slipped through his fingers.

Her eyes burned bright as she got back to her feet. The portal shone bright behind her, sharply defining the contours of her dark silhouette. A gush of wind blew her scarf and hair back, save for a rebellious red strand that flew over her face. She raised a hand to force it back behind her ear. The tip of her fingers were as red as the lock of hair.

Ms. Wada came at Yukina from behind, hard and fast, the dagger held out in front of her.

The young woman cried out in agony as she fell onto the soggy ground, more from the momentum of her attacker's charge than the actual cut. Ms. Wada let out a long stream of furious Japanese as she changed her grip on the dagger. She raised it Psycho-style to move in for the kill, but Yukina was as fast as ever. No sooner had she hit the ground than she rolled onto her back, a maneuver she finished off with a kick to Ms. Wada's chest. Unlike the *shikome* I tried that attack on, it sent our would-be killer flying backwards with a satisfying crunch. Her now-broken nose left an airborne trail of blood the whole way down.

A series of shots came at us from the left. Kung's men had found their firing positions. Kennedy laid down some cover fire as I slithered to get out of the way of the bullets. Along the way, I grabbed the Glock the guy Yukina gutted had dropped. Be damned if I was going down without trading a few shots of my own.

I crawled my way to the next gravestone over. Time had worn it down to the point of illegibility, but it was still solid and high enough to crouch behind. Sticking the knife in the dirt blade-first, I poked my head around the right side to see where the muzzle flashes were coming from. I counted five guns when a sixth one went off a lot closer.

Kung had pulled out what looked like my Sig to send shots Kennedy's way. He was taking cover behind a tree of his own; too bad it left his back exposed to me. Three mini-geysers of blood mist popped from his shoulder blades as I pulled the trigger. He staggered out of cover from the shots, leaving himself wide open. As I was lining up the *coup de grace*, Kennedy landed the kill shot to the forehead. It blew him backwards and made him land on his side before he rolled downhill like a human barrel. He landed in the grave Yukina and I had abandoned.

If this were a cheap action movie, this would be the part where the henchmen decide to stop shooting and get out of there. Unfortunately for Kennedy and me, that was the moment they decided to *really* pour on the shots. The SMGs were doing a jackhammer number on my grave, which meant they likely had enough ammo to finish me off after. I looked for new cover that I could get to whenever they ran out of rounds.

One of the guns stopped firing with a strangled cry. Some worried Japanese words were followed by another howl. And another. And another.

Somebody forgot all about Yukina and her sword, I thought. Not that I had much room to speak; I'd certainly forgotten about her in all this excitement. Hearing that made me want to take back everything I said to Lady McDeath about the lack of a credible threat from a sword.

I readied myself to lay some cover fire when I got another ugly reminder of something else I'd forgotten. With a cry, Ms. Wada sliced at my gun hand from the side, making me drop it. Her eyes were wild and unreasoning, her blade raised to slice my throat. I yanked my own knife out of the ground with my left hand, instinctively planting it in her solar plexus. Her eyes grew wide as the pain of the blow sunk in, making her look down at my bloody hand clutching the equally bloody hilt. She forgot all about her own blade, letting it drop as she wandered away from me and towards the grave where the portal was.

She stumbled up to the gateway, her hands clutching my knife as if that could stop the waterfall of blood staining her formerly white robe. When she was in front of it, she fell to her knees and said something in a halting tone. It sounded like the same language she'd used to open the portal in the first place.

Yukina strode up to her from the shadows, her own very bloody blade in hand. Her eyes drew appreciative as she noted the stance the woman now crouched in. Ms. Wada herself only had eyes for the portal as Yukina came up behind her. My partner raised her sword into position, held that pose for a second, before she brought the blade down on the blonde's neck with one clean sweep.

The headless body fell back on top of Kung's fresh corpse while the head itself flew in my direction. It landed right in front of my bullet-battered gravestone, mouth open as wide as the eyes. When I looked up again, Yukina was removing my knife from the corpse she'd made.

The vigilante stood back up and turned to face me. She was about to join me when a sound froze her in place. A low thrum came from the portal, which was swirling faster and faster as it widened.

"Shit!" I sprung back to my feet as something the recently-beheaded woman said floated back into my mind.

"I imagine two lives will truly whet her appetite."

I turned my back to the portal but it was too late. A discharge of pure energy blasted out of the portal with a loud *boom.* The beam pulsed as it spat out wave after wave of energy.

Out of the corner of my eye, I saw Yukina thrown away by the sheer strength of it. She was forced to roll backwards so she could regain her footing. The shockwaves kept me from getting any closer too. I was still struggling to push my way through when the first arrivals from Yomi responded to the accidental dinner invitation.

19

SKIN AND BONES

The first guests to show up were the *shikome*; it's not like Izanagi's palace wasn't full of them or they hadn't intended to investigate the other side of the portal anyway. Six of those ugly hags glided on the crest of that invisible power wave. They only had eyes—and fingers—for the exposed Yukina, who resumed her fighting stance. Her eyes flared with a hatred that scared me almost as much as the portal...Almost.

Even from this far away, I could see the difference between this fight and her last tangle with the *shikome*. Before, she'd barely held her own against two of them. Now, she handily, almost disdainfully, blocked every strike six of them had to throw, weaving her sword strikes into an unbreakable web of steel.

Kennedy ran out from her tree, making a beeline for where Kung's men lay. "Ah, hell no!" she yelled while tossing shots at the demonesses in our midst. Most of them went wild but one caught the middle *shikome* in her left hand. That was all the opening Yukina needed to take its head from its shoulders.

A couple of the Divine Mother's minions broke off to go after Kennedy. Too bad the Texas-born reporter was ready for them. SMG fire stopped them cold in their tracks, pushing them back with controlled bursts in the same way the power wave was keeping me back from the portal. Meanwhile, Yukina took out the knees of the one closest to me and was battling the other two to a standstill.

Deciding my reporter friend had the right idea, I scrambled back behind the gravestone to grab my Glock.

I won't say it was easy getting closer. Enough rain hit the ground to turn the whole place into a mud pit. Between the lack of traction and the continuing outpouring of energy from across the border, it was all I could do not to fall down myself. Still, I was able to bring up the Glock into a decent firing position and shoot.

I hit the nearest standing hag with my first shots, starting from the side of her foot and working my way up to her shoulder. Yukina took advantage of the distraction to cut the other *shikome* into two pieces at gut level. The torso was still in the air when she turned her sword on the shot *shikome* and cut her right down the middle. I kept shooting at the crippled *shikome* until my traveling companion could finish her off with another guillotine maneuver.

I glanced over at Kennedy's position. One of her attackers had fallen over, dead, but despite the gunfire Kennedy was pouring at the other one, it drew closer and closer. I emptied the last of my clip into the *shikome's* back, which only staggered it a bit.

"Close the portal!" Yukina yelled at me, using the

momentum of the wave and the mud under her feet to circle around to the last *shikome*. Figure skating could only hope to be that graceful. Within seconds, she was close enough to slice off both arms before taking the head as she zoomed past.

While closing the portal was a good idea, this detective had no clue on how he was going to pull that off. The power wave was too strong to resist, even if I crawled. I needed something else to help anchor me. My eyes fell on the corpse Yukina had speared with her heavy sword. Its brother proved it could cut through chains. Maybe it was stout enough to act as a makeshift walking stick?

Just as that thought crossed my mind, my senses tingled as I felt a darker presence coming through the portal. A big, rotting arm slit through, bringing a hellish stench with it. Christ, I thought the gate guards smelled bad; this scent reminded me of all the times I drove by the local recycling plant. Another arm came out right behind it and both of them made a grab for the portal sides as though it were a doorframe.

With a cry, the eight-foot-tall horror those arms belonged to emerged on our side of the border. It wore a tattered kimono whose color had long since faded into grey. Unlike the *shikome*, its long flowing hair was jet black, covering its face like an escapee from a J-Horror flick. Given what I could see of its body through the holes in the kimono, I was grateful. There was barely any meat on those bleached bones, enough to make the body they were attached to functional.

As it tossed its head back to snarl, I got a clear look at its face and wished I hadn't. I could tell it once belonged to a woman, a stunningly beautiful woman at that. But the tattered flesh on its face hung unevenly over the carefully sculpted skull, letting me see its tongue through its nonexistent cheeks. I was amazed its lips were as whole as they were. If I hadn't seen worse things, I doubt would have handled it.

A hail of gunfire hit it as Kennedy emerged from her position by the grave. The Divine Mother laughed off the shots, which probably hurt about as much as the raindrops. "Do you think your toy is sufficient to cause me harm, little one?" it creaked, scooping up Ms. Wada's headless corpse with one of its bony hands.

Kennedy dodged the swing from the improvised club but lost her footing in the process. She lost her gun too, but the last few seconds proved that wasn't doing her any good anyway.

Yukina took advantage of the distraction to charge the creature from its right side, but the monster saw her coming. A backswing from the corpse club sent Yukina flying. As she skidded onto her back, I was amazed at how she kept a tight grip on her family sword.

So far, it hadn't seen me. Maybe I could use that to my advantage. At least, that was the plan when I ran for the sword still stuck in the other corpse. I was surprised I could yank it out with little to no trouble. I could feel less energy pushback from the statues now its final visitor was loose. It was still strong enough to keep me from reaching them, but they'd have to wait. The priority was the jilted queen who had crossed over.

It was in keeping with my shitty luck that the deity picked that exact moment to spot me. Its sunken eyes flashed with recognition. "You," it growled. "The envoy who trespassed in my domain..."

"Yeah, that's me," I admitted, trying not to look or feel silly holding up my sword with a total lack of grace. "Only now, you're the one doing the trespassing."

The lips split into something that could only charitably be called a smile. "My husband taught me ownership is the right of conquest. And I intend to conquer all."

"So this is all about getting back at your ex?" Kennedy called out. "Girl, move on already!"

"She can't," Yukina said, back on her own feet. "Izanagino-Mikoto has a sacred vow she must uphold, one thousand lives ended every day."

The strange accent was gone and Yukina sounded like she had before we went to Yomi. Her posture wasn't as rigid has it was before. Fatigue had returned on her features and her shoulders slumped a little.

I wondered if the change had to do with the force of the blow. Had it shifted *something* within her?

The Divine Mother looked at the defiant swordswoman with a stare that could peel the paint off a car. "I know you... but from where?"

Yukina's demeanor shifted again. A sneer split her lovely lips as she growled, "I am honored the queen of Yomi would recognize so lowly a personage as one she kept captive in her garden for so long."

Her back straightened and her sword rose into a defensive stance. Her next words, lightly accented, confirmed who was talking. "Misa Asao, sworn companion of Shiro Amakusa."

A horrid choking sound to bubble out of Izanagi's throat. It took a couple of seconds to realize this was the closest she could come to actual laughter. "You say that as though I should fear you. But you children are so prone to misconceptions. The dead woman in my hand thought I would stop with this pitiful nation rather than take the whole world for my own."

"Greedy, greedy," I taunted. "Not even my boss is that aggressive."

The Divine Mother looked at me full in the face. "I think you need a demonstration of what that word means."

She ran at me. What was left of Ms. Wada was raised over her head, ready to drive me into the ground like a tent stake. She was fast and close enough for me not to be able to get out of the way.

I thought I was done for when something tripped her. She fell face-first into the mud and I managed to glimpse the pair of fallen umbrellas her twin sacrifices had left behind. I guessed that my death insurance had renewed and thanked my lucky star.

I jumped on top of the Divine Mother's skeletal shoulders and raced across her back as she slid past. I looked over my shoulder and saw her run into my former cover with a gratifying crack. She growled while leaping back to her feet. I took the hint and kept running towards Kennedy.

"Perhaps you do not fear me," Asao said in Yukina's voice, the vigilante's stance unchanged by all the maneuvers. "But I have doubts about you not fearing *them*."

Something under Yukina's black scarf glowed enough to shine through. I was contemplating the tiny blue light under her neck when the portal yawned wider and became more tangible. A solid stream of ectoplasm came roaring out of it.

"What in the hell is she doing?" Kennedy asked in alarm, raising her gun in self-defense.

I didn't have an answer for her until I saw the stream break up into individual pieces. Each one of them dove into different spots in the graveyard, including that one disturbed piece of earth I'd spotted earlier. "Calling for reinforcements from a pool of souls," I said. "It's time for the return of the angry brides."

Just like that, the spots on the ground burst open like diseased zits finally popping. One by one, female corpses staggered up to Yukina's side in various states of decay. A bright silvery light enveloped them, running along the exposed flesh like second skin. They all wore traditional Japanese bridal dress, and the only thing I saw in their eyes was unbridled rage, the burning desire to dish out some long-delayed payback. As Izanagi got to her feet, she held up her hands in placation. "Please, my children," she begged. "Would you raise your hand against the Mother of All Things?"

"Your hand was raised first," Yukina replied, stepping closer. Now her voice sounded like a mix between herself and Asao. "Cross back to Yomi-no-kuni or these hands shall strike you dead."

All the supplication went out of Izanagi at those words. Another vicious laugh crossed her lips as she lowered her hands. With speed I didn't think she had, she scooped up her corpse club and aimed an upward strike at Yukina's head.

The possessed Yukina was ready for it. Her own skin shone with a blueish tint as she darted back enough for it to miss. She yelled her rage as she charged at the decayed goddess. Her war cry was echoed by the living dead around her who followed her example.

"Does that girl realize she's making this problem worse?"

Kennedy fumed, firing off a few shots from her liberated SMG. I think one of those shots may have bounced off Izanagi's exposed skull.

"She's got our Divine Mother good and distracted," I countered, eyeballing the general melee. "That gives us a chance to solve said problem."

My reporter friend shook her head at me. "Yeah, well, I got me a nasty suspicion our girl may have taken this problem to FUBAR status."

Looking at the portal, I couldn't disagree. Pulling from the pool of souls had stabilized the connection between worlds to the point where it was likely drawing its power directly from Yomi.

"Think you can lay down some cover fire while I see about shutting the door?" I asked Kennedy, adjusting my grip on the heavy sword in hand.

"What the hell you think I've been doing, hoss?" Kennedy retorted as she charged closer to the fight, firing off a few rounds along the way.

Yukina's little maneuver made the repelling force of the statues surge back to life with a vengeance. Every step I took towards the portal grave was like walking through a snowdrift with molasses at the bottom. The heavy sword managed to be a sturdy enough staff to get me to the edge of the grave, but that turned out to be as far as I could go. No matter how hard I pushed, the pushback from the field wouldn't let me in.

My eyes found the fight, which was going a bit better. Yukina was doing her deadly ballerina routine to Izanagi's continual frustration. I had a hard time making out her blink-and-you-missed-it sword strikes, though the flesh each one stripped off the Divine Mother was always obvious. The corpse brides fared worse, too slow and creaky to not get smacked by the club.

Each time one of them was crushed under Ms. Wada's corpse, the spirit that was animating the corpse hatched out of its body like a cracked eggshell. It flew around the eight-foot-tall monster with faster strikes than her own.

Kennedy must have made that connection too, because she stopped shooting at Izanagi and began shooting the animated corpses. As the spirits surged forth, things grew more difficult for the Divine Mother.

It was all very encouraging, but none of this got me closer to the portal. My eyes fell on the tiger statue on my left before going to the sword. It took the right treatment on the blade for the other sword to cut through chains. Could an untreated blade hack its way through marble and painite?

I pushed myself along the edge of the field to reach the statue. As expected, all the energy flying around had effectively anchored the statue into the marshy ground. That let me grab it with my left arm and hang on. Pulling my sword out of the ground, I raised it up before bringing it down on the tiger's neck. I was rewarded with the sight of stone chips flying away on the wave of energy. I did it again, and got more chips.

For some reason, I hummed *"I've Been Working On The Railroad"* as I smashed the sword into the statue again and again. It was everything I could do not to laugh hysterically at what I was doing. Stopping the end of the world by chopping off the head of a priceless artifact with a sword that belonged in the same museum...Irony didn't get any thicker. The same could be said for the marble layer I was hacking my way through. While I was making progress, it didn't want to give.

The sudden cracking came as a shock. As I expected, there was a core of painite under the marble. The tattoo on my back burned painfully as the rare gemstone was exposed. I hacked at it again and a couple of seconds later, the tiger's head flew past me, bashing my cheekbone a little as it did. The force went out of the field instantly and I could reenter the grave area.

The portal reacted to the change, and after a few bursts and sparks, it reversed polarity and started to pull things closer to it.

That didn't help my comrades fight against Izanagi. The liberated spirits were sucked back to the other side of the border, leaving Yukina outmatched again. Kennedy's gun ran out of bullets and she was searching Kung's men for a replacement.

Even in the distance, I could tell Yukina was running out of gas too. Izanagi herself was in rough shape. Her kimono had ripped to the same shreds as most of her flesh. What strips of both weren't on Yukina's blade were scattered all over the muddy cemetery to mingle with the puddles of water.

The Divine Mother still moved as quickly as ever and I didn't doubt a strike from her would kill either of my allies.

Acting on a hunch, I let go of the decapitated statue and let myself be pulled towards the portal. Along the way, I scooped up my Sig from beside Kung's fallen corpse. As soon as I got close to the edge, I stuck the sword back in the ground and yelled, "Kennedy, catch!"

I threw it wide on purpose, factoring in the portal's

attraction, and hoped my calculations were right. It landed a hair's breadth from Kennedy's feet and I smiled.

When I was sure she had it in her hands, I dug around in my pockets. I only hoped Kung's men missed the significance of what I was looking for enough to let me keep it.

Sure enough, my bident was still there, waiting to be used. The two-pronged piece of painite was a comforting weight in my hand. Normally, I'd think twice about using Lady McDeath's tool for talking to the dead in a way other than it was intended, but this was anything but a normal situation.

Acting out of instinct alone, I jammed it into the portal, sticking my left arm all the way in up to my elbow. It hurt. I felt my hand burn and blister, like I'd decided to dip it in an active volcano, which I guess was close enough a description.

I screamed as all of me seemed to burn in unison with my arm. All the cuts and bruises from the past hour were like a hundred hot needles piercing my skin. The tattoo on my back burned like it was on fire. The pain nearly made me lose my grip on the sword but I tightened it out of sheer stubbornness. The whole world depended on me getting this right.

I had only one thought left in my mind. *Painite controls the portals and I control the painite.* Focusing beyond my screaming nerve endings, I poured my borrowed powers into the bident. Once I felt like I had a connection with it, I concentrated on making the portal smaller to the point of being shut.

The light was so bright, my vision went white, but I pushed on. Though I couldn't see it, I could feel the portal pulsing in front of me. I could feel its energy in my mind and used my will to fight it back. I fought on, gritted my teeth as I pushed back, my hand still clutching the bident. I used all of my strength, throwing my emotions into the mix. My pain, my hopes, the thought of all the lives that hung in the balance... A primal scream escaped my throat as I took a step forward, then another.

I couldn't feel my hand anymore except in terms of the energy being sucked into the bident. As the portal closed around my arm, I felt something give way. It reminded me of whenever my stomach lurched two seconds before I threw up. With a major effort, I yanked my arm out of the portal right before it sealed itself off with a pop.

The night was dark again, and I had to blink several times before I could make out the tip of my shoes. When I saw what had happened to my hand, I couldn't help but stare. The skin was torn down to the dermis level and even the dermis was as tattered as Izanagi. A skeletal hand was now holding my bident. I watched, amazed, as the bony fingers opened to reveal the carved painite. I grabbed it with my good hand and stuffed it back in my jacket pocket.

I flexed my fingers open and closed again, marveling at the sight. It didn't hurt anymore and though I was no doctor, I was certain what I was seeing was impossible. But the digits obeyed my commands as easily as if they hadn't been stripped to the bone.

A woman's cry behind me had me looking over my shoulder. The fight with Izanagi was still raging and my heart sank. Sure, I'd sealed the Divine Mother away from the source of her power, but she still had enough fight in her large frame to drive Yukina and Kennedy back. The few spirits still floating around were practically translucent.

Cutting them off from the pool in Yomi had to be weakening them as well.

I tried getting back to my feet and the world whirled dangerously around me. Everything hurt, nearly making me pass out from the agony. I lifted my head to the sky and opened my mouth to make the scream I couldn't get out.

A peculiar thought hit me as the raindrops washed down my face. Water...water was the source of all life. That made it the antithesis of death, which Izanagi now personified. There was something about it, a soothing calmness to the drops that cascaded over my battered body. And a connection I didn't understand, but that I could feel growing in the back on my mind, washed over me. It was like the gut feeling that had pushed me to use the bident to close the portal. I had no idea where it came from, but I knew better than to ignore it.

My clothes were soaked and rain had pooled around my feet. The drops came faster and closer together as the rain intensified. It washed away the grime and blood from my face with a cleansing touch.

Turning my face to the angry skies again, I opened my lips to let the drops pass through my parched lips. Fire. Earth. Air. And the source of life... Water.

One of the most powerful of the four element, it has a will of its own and a relentless strength. Water cannot be stopped and always finds a way... Without more thought, I reached up into the stormy skies with my mind and...*pulled*.

The rain went from a heavy shower into a blinding downpour. The skies crackled and sparked as lightning and thunder joined in. The wave of water falling on me was reinvigorating and I bathed in it gladly. I could feel its power all around me and something in my veins sang alongside it.

I balled my bony hand into a fist and did the same with the other one. My feet seemed to glide across the muddy ground as I strode over to the Divine Mother.

Izanagi herself wasn't having the same luck. The ground had turned into a swamp under her feet. She sank up to her ankles in it, to the point of being unable to walk. That didn't stop her from swinging what was left of Ms. Wada's corpse, which was reduced to her pelvis and legs. When she raised it to try to hit the barely-standing Yukina, a couple of shots rang though the falling skies. A small mist of blood sprang out of her club-wielding wrist, making the fingers snap open and drop her bludgeon. The goddess screamed in agony at the shot.

I wondered how Kennedy was able to injure her. Maybe all the previous blows had worn her down. Maybe being cut off from Yomi had turned Izanagi's god-mode off. Either way, her lowering her arms gave me all the opening I needed.

I grabbed the weakened goddess from behind in a bear hug, my uninjured hand wrapping around the wrist of my tattered one. The crazed monster raged and fought against my grip but I had more than enough strength to keep her arms by her side. When she tried to yank her feet free of the mud, I aimed my foot at the back of her left knee. It took a couple of kicks but she went down on it and then the other one when I knocked it out from under her.

As soon as she was kneeling, I got a glimpse of the remaining brides spirit through the curtain of rain. They poured into Yukina's extended blade, making it light up with the same blue I could see running along her skin. Izanagi tried to fight me in earnest at this point; I guess she could feel her end was coming and she wanted nothing to do with it.

Yukina raised her sword in the same execution pose she had with Ms. Wada. She gave me a look that only had one message: "Move."

I obeyed and ducked my head. The Tsing family blade came down swiftly, separating head from shoulders in a single blow. The Mother of All Things went limp in my arms, prompting me to drop her. Her head, on the other hand, went rolling down towards the grave, stopping right next to the decapitated statue of the tiger.

Yukina stood in front of me, soaked to the bone. Her hair and clothes were plastered to her battered body. There were several cuts along her arms and legs and I could see blood mingling with the raindrops. As I watched, I realized I had no idea who stood in front of me now. Was it the young woman I met in Little Japan or the prisoner I released in Yomi? And who had dealt the *coup de grace?*

I felt my arms grow weak and the rain ceased almost completely. A few scattered drops kept falling, but it was nowhere near as heavy as before. Kennedy ran up to me, holding up a hand to my torso to keep me from falling over.

"What'd you do this time, ya damn fool?" she admonished me, giving my hand a worried look.

I managed to give her a grin. "The usual...Helped save the world."

She draped my uninjured arm around her shoulder and took most of my weight. "Just a simple heist, you said. Get in, get out," she tsked. "Hoss, you've got some 'splaining to do."

Ahead of us, I saw Yukina freeze and then turn sharply

around. A whole crowd of ghost brides appeared before her, paler and more translucent than before.

I nodded at Kennedy to get us closer, and she obeyed without a word. The ghostly brides swayed in the night hair, their bare feet floating a few inches above the ground. As we neared Yukina, I could see every one of them had an expression of peace on their faces. As one, they bowed before Yukina. Drawing herself to her full height with difficulty, the vigilante gave the bow back. The brides faded away as they straightened back up. As they flickered into nothingness, the skies above us cleared, showing off a few stars.

"Are they... free?" I asked Yukina.

"Yes, they are—" She froze, turning her head to the side with a frown. Distant sirens were coming our way.

I shook my head. "Figures somebody in this neighborhood was bound to find a working phone eventually," I groaned.

"Good thing I still got a getaway car round the side," Kennedy said. "That is, if you two are done taking chances for the night?"

Yukina nodded, still able to walk but worn down. "More than done," she agreed.

Kennedy dragged me to the side exit while Yukina took point. By the time the first patrol car rolled up to Pineshadow's entrance, we were well on our way.

20

LINGERING EFFECTS

The middle-aged Japanese couple was laughing as they came through the front door of their home. The suit and cocktail dress told me they'd been out to a very nice restaurant, far more upscale than the Emperor's Palace. The laughter cut off instantly at the sight of Kennedy sitting on the couch.

"Mr. and Mrs. Watanabe?" she asked casually as if she were sitting in a café instead of their home.

"What is the meaning of this?" Mr. Watanabe asked with all the indignity he probably gave a waiter who'd messed up his order.

My reporter buddy gave him that razor-sharp smile I'd come to know oh so well. "Candice Kennedy, Full Access News...I wanted to talk to you about some transactions you made with one Mr. Lao Kung, alleged crime boss of Little Japan."

"We have nothing to say to you," Mrs. Watanabe spat,

whipping out her cell phone. I wasn't sure if she was going to take a picture of Kennedy or call the police. Either way, Yukina's sheathed katana slapped the phone out of her hand from behind.

The not-so-happy couple blanched at the sight of Yukina in her full Avenging Woman gear, right down to the scarlet scarf over her nose and mouth. Mr. Watanabe reached into his pocket, which was my cue to step out of the shadows next to the door and stick the Sig P226 in his ribs.

"Careful," I purred into his ear. "We'd like to keep this interview civilized. But if you do anything stupid, there will be consequences."

"And I'm sure you know which kind," Yukina added, her eyes darting between the two of them.

"So why don't y'all take a seat?" Kennedy finished, her voice as pleasant as ever.

I patted down the man of the house's pockets and found the 9mm Berretta he was reaching for. I took a couple of steps back and stuffed it in the waistband at the small of my back while I gestured at our hosts to sit down in front of Kennedy. They obliged me without any fuss. Still, I made sure they could see the Sig I kept aimed at their heads.

"Now then," Kennedy went on as Yukina stalked her way to the opposite side of the Watanabes' seats. "We have rock-solid evidence you made large transfers of cash to the account of the late Mr. Kung."

"Impossible," Mrs. Watanabe scoffed. "We donated those amounts to charity."

"Charities which only exist on paper." Kennedy glanced down at her phone. "See, I have this friend who's quite the computer expert. He's gone and done some digging and found they're fronts for Kung's organized crime. Now, given all that loot from the museum that was found in Kung's car, I bet it won't take the cops very long to find out as well."

"Let us allow that these organizations are fraudulent," Mr. Watanabe said, his face assuming the expression of someone negotiating a delicate business deal. "That does not mean we are criminals ourselves."

Yukina made a dramatic gesture that removed the cover from her sword. "I beg to differ."

"Your son died in a car accident recently, didn't he?" I chimed in. I was glad to see Kennedy's idea of round-robin questioning was keeping them off-balance. As long as each of us asked questions, they wouldn't be able to focus on any one of us as the spokesperson.

"What does this have to do with our private finances?" Mrs. Watanabe asked, pretending not to get it, but I could see the fear in her almond-shaped eyes.

"He was a fairly young guy, just twenty-two," Kennedy stated, ignoring the question. "Our condolences, by the way..."

"But would your son have wanted you to purchase him a living bride now that he is dead?" Yukina continued.

Mr. Watanabe laughed derisively. "Are you insane? We got him a doll, like we are—"

"That's for peasants, not a noble house like yours," I interjected, fighting my urge to shoot him. "Traditions have to be followed to the letter, don't they?"

While both of them seemed a little scared by my words, panic hadn't settled in yet. I could see the husband's eyes repeatedly darting to the side of the room, and it brought a smile to my face.

"What do you keep looking at?" I asked, as I took a step closer to an ancient vase. "This?" I pushed it with the barrel of my gun and watched as it shattered to the ground. The removal of the pottery revealed what was hiding beneath its base: a round plastic button.

Something that was undoubtedly a curse passed through the Japanese man's clenched teeth.

"Sorry, my bad," I said, amused, before pressing down on the button with a flourish. The fact nothing happened was sort of anticlimactic.

That's when Yukina pulled the rug out from under them. "I wouldn't rely on your silent alarm helping you."

"Now don't get us wrong," Kennedy said. "It's part of an impressive security system. It's just we know somebody who's a king at breaking 'em."

"And since no cavalry's coming to help you out of this," I said, crossing over to be closer to Kennedy, "it's time for you to make a choice."

"Tell us where she is and we go," Yukina said. "Refuse and you will never leave this place alive."

The sheer powerlessness of their position sank in with her words, yet still the Watanabes seemed reluctant to come to the table.

"How about we sweeten the pot?" Kennedy suggested. "Seeing as Kung is dead and all, we could give you a full refund of what you paid him."

"Of course, that also means turning state's evidence in every one of Kung's crimes you two are an accessory to," I added. "That money's going to come in very handy when it comes to paying the lawyers."

"And how is this a good deal for us?" Mrs. Watanabe asked indignantly.

That's when I pulled out my ace-in-the-hole. I took my still-skeletal hand out of my pocket and pointed towards the ceiling. "Because there are worse things than being dead."

Both husband and wife recoiled at the sight and I couldn't blame them. My hand was better than it was a few nights ago, but a long way from healed. Most of my forearm had healed, the burned skin growing back layer by layer. But my hand had remained skeletal, and I had a feeling it would stay that way. I knew I shouldn't be able to move the bones without tendons and muscles, but each one of my fingers still behaved as they did before I shut the portal.

"And disgraced," Kennedy added, her sweet tone taking on a harder edge. "If you make us go that other way, I'll make it my business to air out every last stocking of dirty laundry after you're dead and gone."

Mr. Watanabe stroked his chin as if he were weighing the options on a restaurant menu. His eyes tracked every movement of my skeletal hand. "If we do all this, we will get the money back?"

"Their word is my word," Yukina said under her mask. "Ask your grandmothers in Little Japan what the word of the *fukushuu onna* is worth."

The couple exchanged a glance and Mrs. Watanabe said, "The girl is in the basement. She would have been... processed by now but with what happened to Kung, we—"

Yukina's katana at her neck made her stop talking. I held out my skeletal fingers. "Key?"

Mr. Watanabe nodded and pulled out his keyring. He tossed it at me, rather than lay the keys in my open skeletal palm.

———

Even though it'd been a few days, there was no mistaking the girl Yukina and I saw under Little Japan's streets. She was a lot more animated than the last time we saw her.

She drew back in fear at the sight of us in the doorway, crawling away as much as her zip-tied hands and feet would let her. She was sitting on a cot, a thin blanket wrapped around her shoulders. Though she looked terrified, she seemed unharmed.

Yukina pulled down her scarf so the girl could get a look at her face. She talked to her in soothing Japanese as she cut the zip ties with a dagger. As soon as the girl's hands were free, she threw her arms around the Avenging Woman, saying a burst of Japanese so rapid and buried in tears to have no real translation.

After getting the girl to her feet, Yukina said, "Let's go."

I nodded, careful to keep my left hand in my pocket as we made our way back to the ground floor. I was sure Kennedy was finished putting the now-unconscious Watanabes on the couch she'd been sitting on.

———

A few blocks away, a gypsy cab rolled to a halt in front of us. Yukina had secured the blanket around the girl's shaking shoulders and we'd since removed the bride headgear from her head.

"I...I don't know if I can go back to the dorm," she said, shivering against a fear worse than basement-induced cold.

"It's safer than Little Japan," Yukina assured her. "And I'll be keeping a close eye on you for the next couple of days."

"And I can make sure the public keeps a few more of them on you if you want," Kennedy offered.

She looked at all three of us and asked Kennedy, "Could I ride with you? You're famous. They wouldn't attack somebody famous."

She chuckled as she gave her a hug. "Well, if anyone does, honey, I'll shoot the fucker."

"We'd better get moving," I said. "We don't know how long that all-natural sedative Mao gave us will last."

Yukina and I said our goodbyes to Kennedy and the girl. The cab pulled away while we walked in the direction of Little Japan.

After a block went by, I said to Yukina, "Don't you think now would be a good time to explain the Asao situation?"

I saw a flicker of Asao pop up on her face but not take it over. "What is to explain?" she asked.

"How about that blue glow I saw that night?" I answered. "It looked a lot like how some of your uncle's flashier charms work."

Asao went away from Yukina's face as she pulled out a hacked off piece of bamboo from her pocket. Some intricate symbols were carved on it that looked a little cruder than Mao's handiwork. "I had to make this on the fly," she explained. "The *dotanuki* cut the bamboo and my needle did the carving. It's the only charm I ever really learned from my uncle."

"What does it do?" I asked as we turned the corner. Evening traffic zipped by us and we were the only pedestrians on this stretch of sidewalk.

"Calls for the aid of spirits," she explained. "I meant to use it as protection, to get the souls from the pool to help. But when Asao died in my arms in Yomi and his spirit had nowhere to go... I didn't expect the possession—"

Her features tightened as Asao took over. "Neither of us did—"

Then she became herself again. "But that may have been because I *was* in Yomi. It worked the way it should for the brides. But now Asao is sort of stuck with me." She shrugged. "Or me with him."

"And how do you feel about this situation?" I asked with more than a little concern.

Yukina tilted her head to the side. "It's...unique. We're ourselves and yet we're also something..."

Asao came over her face as she said the last word, "...more...*fukushu no seishin*...an avenging spirit."

I took a long look at her. Everything from her face to her stance seemed to indicate she was alright with the situation. "The Avenging Spirit," I smiled at her. "Yeah, it does have a certain ring to it."

She chuckled in response.

"And you're okay with the whole body-sharing situation?" I asked.

"I could not put it into words, but it works. We are joined at a level that runs so deep, it feels as if he were here all along."

"And what do you think of this century and place so far, Asao?"

Asao nodded their head with appreciation. "Some things are very different. Some things are depressingly familiar. But all in all, it is a place worth defending. I am proud to call it my new home."

As he spoke, I saw Yukina come back into their face bit by bit. As the last sentence was spoken, both of them seemed to be saying it.

"Does Mao know about this?" I asked. The edge of Little Japan was coming up in the distance.

"He spotted it the second I came back into his shop," Yukina said with a laugh. "He offered to do an exorcism if I wanted."

I sensed more behind her statement. "But...?"

"But I told him what I'll tell you," Yukina asserted. "Whatever the circumstances, Asao proved to be a valuable help. I'm proud and honored to be his vessel."

"Not vessel," Asao asserted through her mouth. "Partner...and the honor is mine."

The Stingray was still parked in the parking lot of the Emperor's Palace, waiting on me to get back.

"What are you going to do now?" I asked Yukina.

"Asao and I are going to Japan," she said with a soft smile. "Did you know, I've never been?"

I shrugged, it wasn't that surprising.

"Asao wishes to return to the land he fought so hard to protect. But we'll come back soon enough."

"Well, if there's ever anything I can do to help either of you, let me know," I said, extending a hand.

Yukina surprised me by giving me a hug. I was too

stunned to react before she let go. She tilted her head to the side, seemingly listening to something only she could hear. "Who knows," she said. "By then, you might be the one who needs our help, envoy."

Her goodbye said, she walked into the crowd of people up the block. She glanced over her shoulder to give me one last cryptic smile before disappearing from sight.

———

I sighed as I got back in the driver's seat. It'd been a hard few days, finding the surviving ghost brides and offering their captors the same deal we had the Watanabes.

The CCPD pinning our heist on Kung had done wonders in persuading them to go along, though. Yukina was good for her word on paying me and Mao was more than happy to throw in some cash himself. That was enough to cover this month's expenses but I knew I'd have to get some more work soon.

All these thoughts went through my head while I started up the car. I put my phone on speaker and dialed up Zian.

The voice that answered wasn't him. "Evening, Mr. Vale. It has been a while, hasn't it?"

There was no way I couldn't recognize that cut-glass British voice. "Hello, Hermes. Am I in trouble?"

The Messenger of the Gods chuckled at my question, which I hoped was a good sign. "I can see why you'd think so, but no, not at present. In fact, I have to commend you for keeping my son as uninvolved in your latest caper as you did."

"It wasn't anybody's choice," I pointed out, pulling out of the parking slot.

"I thank you just the same," Zian's father countered. "I believe thanks are also in order, on behalf of the Conclave, for preventing another ugly border incident."

"Is that what *she* thinks too?" I asked, anticipating Lady McDeath's likely answer.

"Ah. Your benefactor did have some choice words about you entering Yomi, as I recall," he said while I merged with the late afternoon traffic. "That said, I know her well enough to state she is quite glad to see Izanagi-no-Mikoto taken off the chessboard."

"I'm not sure if we're out of the woods yet," I said with a bit of unease. "You'll remember that jinn that snuck over when the last portal opened up."

"Yomi's portal operated off far different mechanics, Mr. Vale," Hermes said with a soothing tone that'd calm a rhino on angel dust. "Even so, I do appreciate your prudent caution in not assuming all is well."

I hesitated for a second before saying anything else. On the one hand, what I wanted to say may have been going out of bounds. On the other, it's not every day you wind up talking to the god whose currency of choice is information.

"Do I have enough pull with you to ask about something personal?" I said, the traffic dissipating as I put Little Japan behind me.

The Messenger hummed in thought. "Personal in what way?"

"Personal to me," I said, as I glanced down at the skeletal fingers wrapped around the steering wheel. "I'm guessing you know about my hand."

"I do, although I am curious as to how it happened."

Hermes remained silent after I finished recapping how I closed the portal. When I asked him if I was getting my old hand back, the words he said to me were ones I doubt he used often. "I do not know Mr. Vale. No one such as you has ever done what you did. Were you not an envoy under the protection of my uncle, I fear you would not have survived at all."

Fat load of good that answer did to me. "Not that I don't appreciate being alive, but I was kind of attached to my old hand, you know. Isn't there something I can do to get it back to the way it was?"

"I would suggest..." Hermes dragged the answer out "...you invest in gloves."

I bit back the nasty retort that was on the tip of my tongue, because Zian's father scared the shit out of me on the best of days.

"Thanks. How about what happened afterwards?" I asked. "I know I'm bound to your uncle in some way, and I get why I can communicate with the dead and all that. But what I did in that cemetery, it had nothing to do with Hades' powers. So where did that come from?"

"This much I can say," Hermes started, clearly weighing his words carefully. "What happened to you was never meant to be. And there will be a price to pay for it happening."

I sighed in frustration. "You do realize you told me a grand total of nothing or, at least, nothing good."

"I do, Mr. Vale. But it is honestly the most I can offer you...along with this warning. Tread lightly from here on out...We are not the only ones who have noticed these remarkable events."

The phone went dead and I felt an existential dread crowd my guts. What couldn't he tell me? And how bad was it going to get before it was over? I was halfway to my flat before I could find the nerve to call Zian again. The dread of my conversation with his father followed me all the way home.

NOTE FROM THE AUTHOR

Thanks for joining Bellamy Vale's team!

If you loved this book and have a moment to spare, I would really appreciate a short review where you bought it. Your help in spreading the word is gratefully appreciated.

Did you know there are more books in this series?

- Hostile Takeover #1
- Evil Embers #2
- Avenging Spirit #3
- Seasons Bleedings (Christmas Special)

All the books are available in ebook and print.

FURTHER READING

The Neve & Egan Cases Series.

Described by readers as 'a refreshingly unique mystery series'.

- Russian Dolls #1
- Ruby Heart #2
- Danse Macabre #3
- Blind Chess #4

All the books are available in ebook and print. There's also an ebook Box Set, with the complete series, at a bargain price.

ABOUT THE AUTHOR

Cristelle Comby was born and raised in the French-speaking area of Switzerland, on the shores of Lake Geneva, where she still resides.

She attributes to her origins her ever-peaceful nature and her undying love for chocolate. She has a passion for art, which also includes an interest in drawing and acting.

She is the author of the NEVE & EGAN CASES mystery series, which features an unlikely duo of private detectives in London: Ashford Egan, a blind History professor, and Alexandra Neve, one of his students.

Currently, she is hard at work on her Urban Fantasy series VALE INVESTIGATION which chronicles the exploits of Death's only envoy on Earth, PI Bellamy Vale, in the fictitious town of Cold City, USA.

The first novel in the series, *Hostile Takeover*, won the 2019 Independent Press Award in the Urban Fantasy category.

KEEP IN TOUCH

You can sign up for Cristelle Comby's newsletter, with give-aways and the latest releases. This will also allow you to download two exclusives stories you cannot get anywhere else: *Redemption Road* (VALE INVESTIGATION prequel novella) and *Personal Favour* (NEVE & EGAN CASES prequel novella).

www.cristelle-comby.com/freebooks

Printed in Poland
by Amazon Fulfillment
Poland Sp. z o.o., Wrocław

55987788R00143